THE GATES OF POLISHED HORN

A COLLECTION OF STORIES

MARK A. RAYNER

DONOVAN STREET PRESS

Library and Archives Canada Cataloguing in Publication

Title: The gates of polished horn : a collection of stories / Mark A. Rayner.

Names: Rayner, Mark A., 1966- author.

Description: First edition.

Identifiers: Canadiana (print) 20240495411 | Canadiana (ebook) 20240498119 | ISBN 9781999431174

(softcover) | ISBN 9781999431181 (EPUB)

Subjects: LCGFT: Science fiction. | LCGFT: Short stories.

Classification: LCC PS8635.A97 G38 2024 | DDC C813/.6—dc23

markarayner.com

donovanstreetpress.com

First Edition – 2025

Edited by Cal Chayce & Joe Mahoney

Cover Artwork Copyright © 2024 by Bibliofic Designs

For my mother
a seeker at the gates

CONTENTS

ALSO BY MARK A. RAYNER

Novels

Alpha Max

The Fatness

The Fridgularity

Marvellous Hairy

The Amadeus Net

Collections

Pirate Therapy and Other Cures

Two gates there are for our evanescent dreams, one is made of ivory, the other made of horn. Those that pass through the ivory cleanly carved are will-o'-the-wisps, their message bears no fruit. The dreams that pass through the gates of polished horn are fraught with truth, for the dreamer who can see them.

— HOMER, BOOK XIX, *THE ODYSSEY*

SOCRATIC INSANITY

SOCRATES WAS in surprisingly good spirits, considering he was about to die. Of course, the old man was surrounded by friends and family, and even his executioner was solicitous and kindly toward the great teacher.

Grant was trying and failing to contain his excitement. He'd been on many JAUNTS—Jumping Against the Universal Natural Time Stream—but this was the first in which he had been granted permission to attend an important historical event. Up until now they'd restricted his jaunts in time to daily life or historically insignificant occurrences that didn't risk compromising his sanity.

Jaunting was the coolest thing since über-chimping. It had been tightly controlled by the government since its invention because—you know—paradoxes. Not the kind that resulted in ruptures of the universe or massive splits in the timeline, but the kind that turned time travelers into lunatics. There were several whole institutes filled with the insane remnants of early time travel experiments. Turns out it's impossible to change history. The so-called Grandfather

Paradox was resolved categorically, first by physics, and then by experimentation. There was just no way to go back and change history, for a variety of reasons. But it was possible for a time traveler to perceive that they had changed history, and therein lay the danger.

Perception became subjective reality, so returning time travelers really believed they had altered the time stream, even though everything remained the same objectively. There were several thousand nut-job ex-time travelers who believed they had killed Hitler, for example. They believed they'd killed Hitler during their JAUNTS, and in their subjective reality they had, but objectively they hadn't. It just had never taken place. When confronted with history books, documentary footage and Holocaust monuments, these would-be Adolf assassins invariably went off the deep end. Exactly why the cognitive dissonance between their subjective and objective realities often drove time travelers insane remained a mystery—it had been the subject of many a doctoral thesis—but the fact was it did. This is why a very specific set of rules was put in place, and time travelers ignored those rules at their peril.

So Grant knew that he shouldn't do anything to stop Socrates's execution, or say something that might change the history of philosophy. He was there to observe and remember. Anything sent back in time had to be biodegradable or indistinguishable from something that would have existed in that time period because the traveler would often go insane if it wasn't, so he couldn't even take a notepad, though he could take notes on anything he could scare up in the past.

He'd trained for the mission for quite some time. In addition to doing PhDs in philosophy and history, he'd also learned how to record the minutia of events and the long passages of speech he perceived. He could compensate for his brain's inherent flaws and biases through a rigorous discipline known—ironically—as Socratio: a combination of critical thinking, cognitive science, and meditation techniques. He could maintain an almost inhuman detachment from emotion and life in general. These qualities made Grant a staggeringly boring dinner companion. But they helped mitigate the cognitive dissonance that turned time travelers into drooling (albeit well-educated) maniacs on their return to 21st-century Earth.

Socrates was being executed by the authorities in Athens for corrupting the minds of young Athenians, primarily by getting them to question the existence of the gods. His students and friends had gathered to be with him as he was put to death via the ingestion of hemlock poison. He'd already bathed, so the women wouldn't have to wash his body later, and he'd said goodbye to his children.

"Let's do this," Socrates said to his friend Crito.

"So soon? It's not even dusk. Many people don't take the poison until after dark. They eat and drink and make love with their wives. You have time still." Crito tried to keep from crying again.

Grant had already watched the conversation upon which Plato had based his Crito; Socrates's friend had indeed tried to convince the old philosopher to escape prison. And Socrates had explained why he could not do so. Plato had gotten it mostly right, and Grant had to use all his training to push aside a feeling of exhilaration. He needed to watch it play out in front of him without seeming the least bit out of place.

It was hard not to feel bad for Crito. He really loved the ugly old teacher, and he wasn't ready for him to die.

Socrates was ready, though. "Fair enough, but I'm not most men, and doing those things would make me seem foolish in my own eyes. Let's get the poison going!"

Grant felt like he was watching a Monty Python sketch. Socrates actually seemed happy about being killed.

The executioner arrived with the hemlock.

"Gimme," Socrates said, taking the cup from his killer. He lifted the cup and toasted: "To the gods." Then he drank, deeply, finishing it off in one long swallow.

The men gathered there, Socrates's friends and students, philosophers all, began to weep.

"What the serious fuck?" Socrates said. "Why are you crying? How can you be crying at a moment like this? If I wanted crying I wouldn't have sent the women away!"

Despite his training, Grant couldn't help himself; he laughed.

"At least one of you gets it. Who is that anyway?"

Grant tried to control his laughter. The other men were weeping, and Socrates said, "I'm serious, if you don't pull your shit together, I'm going to ask you to leave. You too, giggles.

"This is just the end of my body. Surely our time together will live on. If my words did not survive my mortal flesh, then there would be something worth crying about. Not this." Socrates pinched his own cheek.

Everyone got their emotions under control. The executioner explained that Socrates needed to walk around a bit for the poison to work most effectively. Socrates nodded. He pointed to Grant and said, "Could you help me up?"

Grant looked behind him before realizing that Socrates did indeed want *his* help. That wasn't anywhere in the accounts. Grant's amusement turned quickly to terror. This was dangerous territory. His training helped, but not enough to keep him calm as Socrates threaded his arm through Grant's.

"Let us talk," Socrates said. "I do not know you. Why are you here?"

"To see if the accounts are accurate, sir," Grant found himself saying. It was the stupidest thing he could have said. He should never even hint that he was from the future!

Socrates thought for a moment. "Accounts?" He gazed into Grant's eyes, and the time traveler found himself saying things he shouldn't.

"The written history of your death. We—I—have always wondered. The passages have always been most moving."

"Yet you laughed."

"I didn't expect you to drop the equivalent of the f-bomb," Grant explained.

Socrates looked confused by this idiom, which didn't scan perfectly in Greek. He pondered it for a moment.

"Ah, my profanity."

"Yes. It caught me by surprise."

"They needed to be shaken up. It's important they understand this choice."

"I see."

"Do you? In your world have you conquered the mysteries of death, as you have time?"

"You know I'm not from here?"

"Or you are a madman, but you seem sane, and I don't find it unreasonable that human logic would someday unlock the secrets of the infinite. Can you explain to me why we perceive time as being linear? Is it truly so, or is it the limitations of our senses that make us see time that way?"

"Teacher, why are you talking so long with this stranger whom we have never met and know not?" Plato interrupted.

"Why do you ask questions to answers you know?" Socrates asked Plato.

"So that I may get others to think of the answers, as you have taught."

"Have I?" asked Socrates. The room was quiet, except for Crito, who was still sniffling a bit.

"I've got to be honest," Grant whispered. "I didn't do very well in the mathematics of time mechanics, and all the stuff about closed time-like curves. The short answer is that time is both linear and not."

"This makes me wish I had not taken the hemlock, young man."

"I'm sorry. I wasn't supposed to interfere."

"A wise policy, but impossible to follow, I think. Human nature renders the idea that you would not interfere, in some way, quite idiotic."

Plato had joined them. He nodded.

"Still, the idea is worth considering. But what of the other dangers? Surely some of your cohort would be tempted to change time. To prevent terrible events by ending the lives of those who caused them. Ah, but if events are linear in nature, then what if such a traveler went back in time to slay an evil man, only to discover later that he was an ancestor, say a great grandfather. His great grandfather could then never beget his grandfather, and his grandfather a father, and so the traveler himself could never be born..." Socrates trailed off.

"And thus the traveler could never have gone back in the first instance to kill his great grandfather," Plato finished.

"Exactly." Socrates smiled. "A paradox."

"Yes, we call that the Grandfather Paradox, but it turns out it's not possible to change events in the past. It may seem possible, but when we return to our own presents, the events have never changed. We've run many experiments replicating this. We've stopped trying because it causes time travelers to lose their minds. That's why it's so important that we don't interfere."

"Perhaps it is like you are all prisoners, in a cave, and facing a wall," Socrates said to Grant. "Imagine a torch, lit behind them. They must interpret reality through the shadows cast on the wall. But the travelers have been freed, so they can go outside and see the light. You could see the truth, but all the others, the ones who did not return to the past, are still chained to the wall. They cannot see it."

Plato looked thoughtful at this description of time travel.

"But we still go insane, relative to the others."

Socrates smiled. "That's what many have said of me. Even my own friends, here, don't understand why I didn't defend myself. They don't appreciate why I have taken this poison so willingly, which, as it happens, seems to be working."

Crito sobbed. Plato and Grant helped Socrates return to his bed. As he lay down again, Socrates said to his friends, "You have much to learn from this man, whom we would call mad. But I'd ask that you do not mention his presence here today so that he can have the pleasure of freeing himself from his delusions another way. I call him brave. And interested in the Good. He pursues truth to the edge of sanity."

The executioner returned and checked the progress of the hemlock. Socrates's legs were numb already, and soon his belly was cold. It wouldn't be long now.

Plato was staring at Grant when Socrates said, "You especially, Plato. Do not use your writing against this man. It is a pernicious art.

"Now, Crito, we ought to offer a cock to Asclepius. See to it, and don't forget."

Crito said he would take care of it, but there was no response from Socrates, and everyone in the room burst into tears. Even Grant.

But he was due to return. The vortal would open any moment, and he had to go. But Plato pulled him aside and asked, "Is it possible for me to go with you?"

"What?"

"I would see what becomes of his teachings," Plato said, nodding his head toward the dead Socrates, and all the men mourning him.

Grant didn't know what to say. It was possible, technically, if they sent him back to the same vortal a moment right after Grant. But if Plato went to Grant's timeline, and never returned, then he would never write all his great works, and Socrates would be unknown, and Grant would never come back to witness his death. A paradox that Grant couldn't permit. If he did, then he would go insane.

"No, you can't go with me," Grant said. He felt bad lying to Plato, but it was the safest course of action. "But I can tell you that through your writing, his teachings live on."

"You see, teacher, it is useful!" Plato shouted at Socrates's corpse over the blubbering of the other men. Plato looked ashamed of himself. "My regrets on that outburst. I promise not to share the knowledge, O' temporal transient, but what is your name?"

"Uh..." Grant searched his memory for an ancient Greek name, and couldn't resist saying, "Zeno."

2

WORMAGEDDON

UNTIL THAT YEAR, I dreaded April the most. The cruelest month when the gyre could not hold. A season of rain and humiliation. And worms.

But I'd thought that year would be different. I could feel it in the marrow of my eleven-year-old bones, because that year, I would free myself of the clods. This was what I called the clunky black Oxford shoes that had been the bane of my existence for most of my short life.

In kindergarten, they were no big deal. There was still a glorious *joi-de-vivre* in kindergarten. Need to take off your dress in the middle of class? Why not! Wanna eat the paste? Go for it, man! Mom makes you wear ugly black shoes? We don't care—you're beautiful, baby! But sometime early in first grade, that attitude changed. All of us discovered, in our own ways, the horrible truth: "I'm different and that's bad."

My difference was a minor one—my shoes were weird. But this kind of tiny deviation from the norm can have enormous consequences. I became a figure of fun and teasing for at least a few minutes of every day that I had to wear that hyper-functional footwear, every time we were at recess or gathering for class.

I had one brief respite from the embarrassment of those shoes: the year my family moved from Canada to live in Britain. I was sent to a state school where the food was terrible, the teachers were mean, and most of my classmates were football hooligans-in-training. But did I care? No, because everybody was wearing clods, so I didn't stand out. My "American" accent was distinctive, but that was one of those rare differences that made people like you.

While abroad, I picked up their accent so upon my return I had another season of being the schoolyard novelty. The strangeness of my English accent meant the black Oxfords went practically unnoticed. Over the winter, my dialect reverted to that of everyone else, and my reprieve was over.

At that point in my life, winter was my favorite season. It was the great equalizer in terms of footwear. In the 1970s we hadn't heard of climate change, and it was a season of boots. A snowscape gloriously free of the clods.

In those days, my best friends were Jason and William. We called William Wild Bill. Jason was a quiet, athletic kid who did well in school, and generally didn't get noticed, either for good or ill. When Bill and I would get into scrapes, Jason tended to stay out of the fray, and neither of us could really blame him for it (though secretly I hoped he would fully join our triumvirate of trouble and take the odd bloody nose for me).

Wild Bill was an unrepentant maniac. His difference was obvious and visible—a large birthmark that covered his right ear and a big part of his neck. The invisible problem was that his dad was a drunk, a bully, and as we used to say back then, a "complete a-hole." Bill was smart, and strong, and a consistent target of the bullies at school. That year we were both still too small to stand up to the eighth graders, but we were on the radar of the monsters and their apprentices in seventh grade. We got into our fair share of fights with the younger ruffians, and usually gave as good as we got. We were a team. Comrades and battle-brothers.

That winter Wild Bill invented a game to make the walk to school more fun, which he called "homework curling." Instead of rocks, we used our homework, which for some reason we wrapped in discarded milk bags. (To carry your homework in anything but a milk bag was almost as uncool as wearing clods. There's still no rational explanation for this, except: we were eleven.) The beaten-down snow and ice along the walkways were our impromptu rinks. There was no sweeping nonsense. The object was always distance, and, if possible, acrobatics.

Curling aside, the best part of winter was the boots. Everyone wore them. Well, everyone except for the eighth graders. They were the monsters of the playground, leviathans that wreaked havoc on lesser lives the way that Godzilla could ruin your shopping trip to downtown Tokyo. In winter they did not deign to notice the ice and snow and came to school wearing their brand name running shoes—Adidas. I vowed that someday I would have a pair of Adidas, and wear them in the winter too, dammit. This was sheer bravado. Mom would never let me out of the house wearing shoes in winter. I could get away with stuffing my hat in my parka pocket before I arrived in front of the school-yard, but that was as far as I was likely to take it.

Throughout the winter of sixth grade, I lobbied hard to get rid of the Oxfords. Mom was impassive, but Dad was somewhat sympathetic to my plight. As a boy, he'd had bright red hair and had suffered under the Godzillas of his day too. The main resistance from my mother was that as a youngster I'd had a slight problem with my gait, and she wanted to make sure I had enough arch support to correct it. Well, my walking was five years corrected, and even with the reprieve of living in England it seemed like a lifetime of suffering. In late March, she finally agreed: If we could find running shoes that had good arch support, I could wear them to school.

The only shoes that fit the bill—that weren't clods—were stiff leather Adidas. I couldn't feign disappointment. I was one happy little dude.

So, it was April. It was lovely. There was no hint of cruelty in the air, just the damp fecundity of worms as they came out of their earthen holes to experience the rain. The center could not hold them, and I'd always liked watching them stretch and move. They were fascinating, but I wasn't the kind of boy that needed to pick them up or, even worse, eat them. According to Jason, Wild Bill had been a prolific worm-nibbler in his early days before my family ever came to the neighborhood. Jason shared my live-and-let-live attitude toward the worms, but Wild Bill maintained a visceral (if not digestive) interest in the poor creatures. He stomped on the bigger ones and ignored the tiny, spaghetti-like worms as we walked to school in a light rain.

Despite the rain, I'd insisted that I debut the new shoes, and Mom finally acquiesced when I explained that I wasn't going to get them wet. They were the best shoes I'd ever had—how could I get them wet? It was unthinkable. Don't worry, I'd said. They'll be okay.

I was true to my word. Jason, who was wearing rubber boots, stomped in the occasional puddle while Wild Bill enthusiastically committed squirmicide. I stayed on the straight-and-narrow, studiously avoiding any contamination of my brand-new Adidas. They were white with blue stripes. They were cool. I was wearing something cool. Jason noticed them but didn't say anything. Wild Bill may have noticed but if he did, he didn't let on.

We arrived too late to play in the yard, so we went straight to class for an exciting morning of repeating things. It was math, my worst subject, but I didn't care. While we recited the times tables, the skies opened up outside, and it rained hard. Cindy McLeish, who sat next to me, sighed heavily while we copied stuff in our notebooks.

"What's wrong?" I asked. It might have been the first time I'd asked a question like that, openly solicitous of another person's feelings. But I was in an effusive mood.

"At recess, there'll be worms," she whispered, almost inaudibly as she tried to escape the notice of Mrs. Walsh's superhuman hearing.

"You don't like worms?"

"No!" She stopped as Mrs. Walsh roused herself from the book she was peering at. A dangerous moment passed as Walsh scanned the classroom, looking for the source of the outburst. "No. I hate worms. They're disgusting," she whispered with feeling. "I especially hate it when the boys whip them at the girls."

Cindy had a bit of a lisp, almost undetectable now because she'd had two years of speech therapy to disguise the blemish on her normalcy. She also had curly blonde hair and bright blue eyes that I'd never really noticed before. She was kind of pretty, I thought at that moment. And the way she said "wormths" was cute. These were odd and novel thoughts.

"I won't throw them at you."

She looked at me and smiled. "Really?"

"No. Especially if you don't like it."

"Thanks," she said quietly. "By the way, I like your shoes."

I beamed a smile at her instead of saying anything, which was good because Mrs. Walsh was watching us over the hawk-like beak of her nose. We were one word from detention. As I smiled at Cindy, I was acutely conscious of two things: Cindy was smiling back at me, and Wild Bill was watching this whole exchange with incredulity. He was staring at me, asking me, as if by telepathy, "What are you nuts? You're talking to a guuurl!" His accusation distracted me. If I'd been able to fully absorb that moment, it could have saved me years of frustration when it came to the opposite sex; I might have learned a valuable maxim: Women care about shoes. They notice them. It matters what you have on your feet. It's a lesson that took me another thirty years to absorb.

At recess, there were, indeed, worms. Lots of them.

In the annals of childhood, I doubt that there had ever been—or ever will be—such an orgy of worm-hurling.

Cindy and I got there late, as we were pulled aside by Mrs. Walsh, who had actually heard our whole conversation and wanted to let us know that she was not pleased. She wasn't going to make us stay inside at recess though. A warning was enough.

No warning could have prepared us for the horror of that recess. We walked outside in the fresh April air, my feet resplendent in their new Adidas, to a scene of rampant worm-whipping debauchery. The girls squealed in disgust as the boys chased them, their hands slippery with worm goo and the creatures themselves. Wild Bill was a central figure in this slimy saturnalia as he gleefully directed other boys to "really fat ones" and chased Amy Menderson around the yard with a handful of the poor creatures. Had the worms the capacity, they would have been, no doubt, troubled and confused by their sudden aeronautics.

Of course, now I realize that the act of whipping a worm at a girl could either be construed as the worst of outrages or the most flattering thing a boy could do. Amy Menderson was squealing, but I'm sure now it was only half in disgust.

Cindy took one look at the chaos and froze in the doorway. I stood with her and tried to talk with her about horses—I vaguely remembered that she liked them, but in that moment of horror she wasn't much of a conversationalist. For the most part she just observed the goings-on with the anxious watchfulness of a meerkat. Her eyes were just as big.

Near the end of recess, Wild Bill had finally tossed his penultimate worm, and he called me over.

"What's up?" I asked.

He had one left in his hand. He showed it to me. "For you."

"Yeah?" I laughed. I was nervous. He had that look in his eye, the one that he got right before he committed some kind of atrocity.

"Yeah. To throw at Cindy."

He was testing me, and I guess I failed in his eyes because I said, "No! She doesn't like it."

"Oh, she doesn't like it," Wild Bill teased. "Well, we better do whatever Cindy says." He proceeded to launch into a rousing rendition of Mark and Cindy "sittin' in a tree, k-i-s-s-i-n-g," loud enough for Cindy to hear, which was brutally embarrassing. When I didn't move to grab the worm, he said, "Fine. I'll do it myself."

"No, Bill, don't."

"What, you gonna' stop me?"

I did not want to fight Bill, especially because we were best friends. You don't fight a best friend over a girl. Or a worm. I looked back at Cindy, who was following the whole conversation, her eyes getting even wider, if that was possible.

Something compelled me to say, "I'll stop you if I have to."

He opened his palm and looked thoughtful. The worm looked pathetic, and on the edge of its wriggly demise. He'd had it in his hand for a while, so it wasn't moving very much. It was starting to dry out. Bill curled his fingers over it, and before I knew what was happening, he threw it on my shoe. My brand new, pristine Adidas.

And then he stomped on it.

There was pain, but more than that, outrage. It was a betrayal of the most inconceivable sort. And the next thing I knew, Wild Bill and I were in a fight that later became known as Wormageddon. I threw the first punch and hit Bill square in the nose, bloodying it. Normally, that would have been the end of a schoolyard fight, but this was more than typical roughhousing.

"Fight, fight, fight!" the gathering crowd shouted.

Bill grabbed his nose and looked at the blood. His face went dark, and he threw a wild haymaker at me. If he'd connected, I'm sure he would have knocked me cold. But his aim was off, and he lost his balance. I pushed him over, still enraged by his betrayal, and was on top of him, punching. He outweighed me, but I had fury on my side. Even so, he got in some good licks, one shot hitting me hard in the eye, which later turned into an impressive shiner. He kneed me in the groin, attempting to lever me off him. He started screaming—a high-pitched screech that was terrifying in its animal baseness. My dismay and the pain from my groin made me hit him even harder. Then he heaved me over, and he was on top of me, overcome with his own rage, pummeling me as I had been thrashing him a moment before. The whole scene was a blur. The kids shouting, fists smacking wetly into my face, into his. There was blood and the sick earthy smell of those damned worms on his hands.

Eventually, Mr. Kovacs arrived to break it up, but it took him and Mrs. Wallace to pull us apart. We were bloodied and even angrier than at the start of the fight.

I looked down, and my Adidas were a ruin, stained with rain, mud, blood, and a trace of the worm gore that had started the whole thing. I would have cried if I hadn't been so furious.

"How could you?" I spat at Wild Bill.

His face was still dark, his birthmark almost glowing with his anger as Mr. Kovacs pulled him away.

"She's a girl," he said. "How could you?"

As they marched us away, Cindy smiled at me. "Thank you," she mouthed, not daring utter the words aloud with everyone listening. By the end of the week, we were "going out," which at that age meant we held hands and were teased mercilessly. (We didn't care. They were just jealous.)

But it came at a cost. You've no doubt heard that when

two boys fight, the cause of the animosity is forgotten almost as soon as the battle is over, but that's only true of a regular fight. This was an internecine betrayal of brother-against-brother; I had sided with a girl, and he had trashed my shoes. I knew he understood what he had done, and I could not forgive him. It was silly. The shoes could be cleaned, and I should have let it go. But I couldn't.

Jason sided with me, and in time we developed other friends. Our circle widened. Wild Bill got a bit wilder. He got taller and stronger. He had lackies, but no friends, and I thought he seemed lonely. By eighth grade, he was the undisputed king bully and everyone was terrified of him. Even me, who had come to a draw with him in Wormageddon. But he had his growth spurt way before I did, and I knew he could whip me if he wanted to. He never picked on me, though. I'm not sure if that was because he'd forgiven me for my betrayal or because he regretted his.

Cindy and I "broke up" even before our bruises faded.

Walking the dog an April evening forty years on I'm reminded of Wild Bill as rain brings out the worms, glistening on the sidewalks. I think of how I left him, alone, to become our schoolyard Godzilla.

And I wonder, could I have been the monster, not him?

3

LOVE'S LACUNA

"I ALMOST DIED the night I was born. Did I ever tell you that?"

"Yes Oscar, you've told me. Many times." It was the central topic of their relationship, Oscar's brushes with death. They talked about that more often than about their wedding. Liz wondered why they had bothered with a wedding in the first place. Her understanding was that couples got married so they'd always have something to fall back on during conversational lulls, but in their case it seemed kind of superfluous.

"I was born the night before the first referendum in Quebec."

"Yes, you told me the story, sweetie."

"I know but it is a good story, right?"

"Yes, if you haven't heard it hundreds of times," Liz said, somewhat exasperated. The agreement had been she would work on her laptop and he would watch hockey. Together time without really being together. "Look, I've got to get this report done, okay? Don't you want to watch the game?"

"Naw. I think I'll go for a walk."

"Be careful."

Oscar smiled. "I always am."

Liz had married him just two years ago but they'd been living together for twice as long. They'd had a glorious, unforgettable fall wedding. She could still see the sunlight in the golden maple leaves, taste the crispness in the air. They'd spent their honeymoon somewhere in the Caribbean later that winter. This was a tropical lacuna. She vaguely remembered landing on the island, the smell of salt air and jet fuel, the sweatiness of the tiny, claustrophobic terminal. And nothing else. Lately, it had been bothering Liz that her honeymoon had been so forgettable.

They'd met in grad school. Oscar had been in the Library and Information Science program, while Liz had been taking her MBA. Both were good programs, but her career had gone better, working as a full-time project manager for a prestigious IT firm, while Oscar was a peripatetic librarian. So far he'd had a total of three part-time positions in libraries around the city, but he didn't seem to mind. Sometimes Liz wondered if that was because he was such a dreamer. On his off-hours he was writing a novel but Liz had yet to see any of it. He promised to show it to her when he had a first draft, but it was four years into their relationship and still no book.

Marriage was not what Liz had assumed it would be. She'd thought that it would make life sweeter but in many ways it just complicated things, made each decision complex in a way that it hadn't been before she'd had Oscar to factor in. Before, it had only been her, an only child, and her parents—and to some extent her paternal grandfather, the patriarch and font of her family's wealth. In Gramps' eyes, the only thing she'd ever done wrong was marry Oscar.

Liz still missed their old apartment near the university where they'd played house and fallen in love. It seemed more real to her, still, than their place in the Beaches. The house had been a gift from Gramps, despite his misgivings about her mate.

She heard the sound of rain outside, and realized the hockey game was almost over. She'd been daydreaming for a couple of hours. How was that possible? She noticed, more and more, that she was having these little episodes. She should ask her doctor about her meds.

The door opened and Oscar came back into the living room dripping wet, his eyes alight.

"If there were zombies everything would be better," he said.

"Better in what sense?"

"More honest and thrilling."

"Right," Liz said, laughing. "Except for all the biting and moaning."

"In the right circumstances, biting and moaning is just what we need." Oscar smiled, and offered his hand.

Liz left the report unfinished and accompanied her husband upstairs.

She awoke to the sound of Oscar uttering a high-pitched moan. Not the groaned hunger pains of the undead, but a cry of panic uttered through the fog of a nightmare.

"Wake up!" She grabbed his impressive bicep and squeezed. Oscar's schedule gave him lots of time to work out, which he did with a set of free weights in the basement. "Wake up, Oscar!"

"Uh... sorry."

"No, don't fall right back asleep. You'll return to it. What were you dreaming about?"

"Hmm. It was like the time I almost died in '95."

"The hockey game?"

She'd heard this story as well, though not as often as she'd heard the birth story. He'd been playing on his house league team when he was fifteen and suffered a really bad concussion.

"I blame Chretien for it being so close."

"What?"

"The referendum."

"I thought another player hit you with his stick."

"No, I took a puck to the temple. My fault, because I wasn't paying attention. I was in the box between shifts and they had a radio on, and I was listening to the results instead of watching the game like Ray Ferraro tells you to."

"Why weren't you wearing a helmet?"

"I took it off so I could hear better."

Liz thought it was strange she'd never heard this part of the story. It was odd that for all these years she'd had the story wrong—not that it changed anything, really. So he'd been hit by a puck, not a stick. And because he'd been listening to the referendum results. It bothered her though, like the phantom pain of an amputated leg, like the way she couldn't tell you much about their honeymoon. Where had it been? The Bahamas or Barbados? She was losing her sense of time. What year had they graduated from their master's programs—had it been the year before their wedding, or the year after?

Had he told her this detail about the referendum before? Maybe he was just making all these stories up. She decided to test him. "What were you dreaming about again?"

"Our wedding. Zombies crashed the party. Ate the brides-maids. And not in a sexy way."

"Ew."

"Yeah, it was pretty hideous. Susan took out a couple though. Did you know she was packing a Glock under that hideous red dress you made her wear?"

"I had no idea. I'm lucky she didn't use it on me. I still feel guilty about those dresses. And they were merlot."

"Red. Merlot. But she plugged a few in the head before they got her. Ripped the dress right off her and then they consumed her face."

"Hmm. I'm not sure how I feel about you dreaming of Susan and her dress being ripped off."

"It wasn't nice. We all died horribly."

"At least they wouldn't have had to listen to your uncle's rendition of Danny Boy. Who sings Danny Boy at a wedding?"

"Drunken Irishmen. Can I go back to sleep now?"

"Fine. Just no more flesh-eating wedding guests. And no more undressing Susan."

"Don't worry, Liz. Yours is the only sweet, sweet flesh I crave."

"Okay, now you're just creeping me out."

───────────

Oscar worked at the main branch of the public library and he liked to ride his bicycle there most days. It was a little thing but it made him feel like a more responsible global citizen. Liz thought it was cute, like most of the ethical decisions Oscar made. Many of them impractical. For instance, he had been a vegan for some time, leading to some ridiculous choices in avoiding animal products. Liz once pointed out that his Crocs were made of ethylene vinyl acetate, which was in turn made out of oil, and guess what oil had once been? The coolness of wearing dinosaurs on his feet had worn off when he realized that everything he did had an impact on the Earth. Also, he'd admitted, he was dying for a cheeseburger.

The bike almost got him killed once as well, she recalled: Her man had been daydreaming, as usual, and didn't check both ways as he went through the intersection. An SUV narrowly missed him and smashed into a car parked at the other side of the road, which woke Oscar out of his reverie. He stopped to see if anyone was hurt. When the driver got out, she was furious at Oscar, even though she had been in the wrong. He might not have double-checked, but he did have the green light. The woman hit him with a tire iron she carried in the car for just such occasions. Luckily, he'd still been wearing his helmet or the driver would have killed him. She did knock him out though.

Liz got to the hospital while he was still in a coma. She was pretty sure it was the only time he'd nearly died while they were together, but he could have been holding a story in reserve.

The evening after his zombie wedding-guest dream she had turned to him and said, "Whatever happened to that woman who tire-ironed you? I remember you went to court to testify."

"Oh, she had to go to an anger management course. She's under house arrest for a year."

"But she could have killed you!"

"Yeah, but she didn't have any criminal record, and the judge thought she'd learned her lesson. We're friends on Facebook now. She feels very badly about what she did, you know. Not being able to drive is making her feel like she's dead."

"Better than her killing someone else."

"Yeah. It's always better when someone's undead like that."

For the first time, Liz really understood that her husband was truly strange. Sexy. Smart. Loving. But fucking weird.

That night she dreamed about zombies. It wasn't the kind she expected. They weren't the rotting, shuffling cannibals of the films; more like lawyers. They roamed her office, hands filled with sheaves of documents, and clipboards they presented to her co-workers. Oscar was there too, watching the zombies spread the forms, and so, spread their plague of paperwork.

When her pointy-haired boss presented a clipboard to her, she balked.

"No forms for me," she told the boss zombie.

"Muhhhh," he groaned, pushing the clipboard at her.

"Up here!" Oscar said. He was sitting like Buddha on the top of a filing cabinet.

The zombie tried to grab her as she escaped her cubicle, and she leaped up to join her husband. Oscar bit her neck, and she awoke screaming.

He wasn't in bed with her, but he came running.

"It's okay," he said. "I wouldn't bite you. Besides, they aren't that kind of zombie."

The next day she couldn't shake a feeling of angst and dread. She was at work when she realized what he'd said the night before. How could he have known what she'd been dreaming?

While she worked that morning, her actual pain-in-the-neck boss seemed less real to her than the nightmare version.

At lunch she went for a walk and time dilated on her, somehow. She snapped out of her Oscar-like trance at their house in the Beaches. She'd walked all the way from downtown. What the hell? She didn't remember any of it. Then she realized the front door was ajar. Had she done that? Or had Oscar left it open? It should be closed. Locked.

She climbed the stairs and went inside. The house seemed cold and eerie. She heard a moan from upstairs. The hair on her neck stood on end and she thought, briefly, that she could just turn the lock on the door and leave. The moan repeated itself. She was drawn upstairs toward the bedroom where she felt it was inevitable that she'd find Oscar having sex with another woman. God she hoped it wasn't Susan. Let it be the tire iron lady. But the bed was empty, still unmade as they'd left it that morning. She noticed a stain on the bed sheets. A wetness, slick and dark. She touched it and was surprised to feel it was cold: some kind of clear fluid. Were they still in the house, hiding? She searched frantically for them, but there was nobody there.

The phone rang. Liz woke up to find herself in bed. Was she dreaming all this? She picked up the receiver. Oscar said, "I'll be home early tonight. I'm making lasagna, with real human flesh!" He laughed like a maniac, and added, "Just kidding. But it will be beef. Now wake up and get back to work." She got up and saw that she was still in her work clothes. She called a cab and went back to the office.

The smell of lasagna filled the house with pungent love. When Liz came in the door, she burst into tears. What the hell was going on? Was Oscar having an affair? She went up to the bedroom, crying, to see the bed was still unmade, just as she'd seen it that afternoon, but now: unstained. There was not even the telltale rim of a stain. It simply hadn't been there.

She took a shower, put on a pair of sweats and a T-shirt, and went down to the kitchen. Oscar sat in a tall stool at the island, reading a book and drinking a glass of red wine.

Without looking up he said, "Have I ever told you about the time we died on our honeymoon?"

4

THE COVERT

THE HIGHWAY only existed a few hundred feet at a time. It flashed by in a series of images, suspended in a dark bubble of night.

The load was a weekly run. And profitable. Like many of the other truckers she knew, she preferred driving at night. The traffic was lighter. It was possible to get better fuel mileage because of that, and if you ended your trip at home, you could spend some time with family or friends during the day. After a sleep, of course.

Her eyes felt sandy and she resisted the impulse to rub them. Grinding salt into a wound. She'd been working for the same haulage company for years now, the time ticking by in a blur of seasons. Her life lived in bursts, suspended in the cloister of her cab.

A deer appeared on the road before her and then it was gone. Did she hit it? There were no vehicles behind her, so she stopped. The truck's hydraulics kicked in and made the tortured sound of commerce interrupted. She opened her glove box and grabbed a flashlight and the .45 Colt she'd inherited from her dad along with the truck and his distant disposition.

She checked the mirror again before she opened the door. It was a secondary highway and unlikely to have traffic on it in the dead of night, but she was still careful about these things. Her dad had drilled safety into her from an early age. After her mother had died, she'd spent all her summer holidays on the road with him. He'd taught her everything she knew about the job. She thought of them as happy times, even though her mom was gone, and she would never see her father laugh again.

She opened the door. As she did, the cab light came on and became a beacon in the night. The decorations were her own, but the red and brown interior was also inherited from her father. The overhead light from the bunk reminded her of all the nights she had slept while her father drove. The comfort she had in hearing him hum along to the radio. The changing of gears and the wheels singing on the road. From a distance, she imagined it would appear like a comfy room, suspended in the night.

She checked the grill and didn't see any blood. Had the deer survived? She sighed and was about to step back into the cab when her peripheral vision caught movement on the other side of the highway, behind some bushes. Her light didn't reach that far, so she walked across the asphalt, black as the horizon. Above her the skies cleared and a few stars appeared.

The deer was lying beyond where she'd spotted the movement. It lay behind a thicket of stunted trees, curled in a crown of grass, a bed, or a nest. It was asleep, apparently. She approached and it didn't wake or startle, and then she thought it must have been dead or knocked unconscious. She kneeled by it and felt its fur; it was warm and rough under her hand. Her palm lay flat on its neck, and she could sense the doe's heart beating. Its breath was soft and steady. She shined her flashlight over its body and could see no signs of injury. It continued to breathe gently and then it raised its head to look into her eyes. They locked, and the trucker felt foolish holding the pistol. She'd come intending to shoot the creature, to end whatever pain she may have caused. Instead, the deer's eyes bore into hers and she heard a voice in her head: It thanked her. It wondered if she knew where the other deer in her herd were.

The doe had been alone for what seemed an eon. In all her searching, she had not been able to find the herd. No scent. No sounds. She'd been walking their pathways for so long. The images came to the driver like a pulse. They were alien and strange, but familiar at the same time.

The deer's consciousness was so limited. Sensations and feelings. Smells were as powerful as sights. And somehow they translated in the trucker's mind. She was suddenly aware of the acrid smell on her—the lubricant in her pistol, the tang of diesel that hung about her. Even her hair smelled of metal and rubber and she was suddenly ashamed of herself.

The deer wasn't judgmental. It just let her know that these were her smells, and for a moment, it was as though the doe and the driver switched awareness.

The driver felt her own hand on her flank. The doe looked down on itself and admired the way the grass curled around her body. It was a good place to sleep, even if it was a bit too close to the road. She felt safe. There was no way to be sure if the moment took seconds or years. But now they could relax.

And neither could know who was sleeping and who was watching.

5

SERVING CELEBRITY

THERE WERE ONLY SO many ways you could cook Hitler.

For all its irony, the Hitler Fusion Stir-Fry was a real flop. So Jeanette Selavy was in a receptive mood when her buyer Mandico Fluridian came in with his latest find.

"This is something so rare you'll want to kiss me for bringing it." Kissing him would have been a challenge. Mandico was a perpetual motion machine made flesh. His head wobbled constantly. If he couldn't do his bobble-head impersonation, his shoulders would shift, he'd snap his fingers or tap his toes.

"We have three stars in the Michelin Guide to think about, Mandico, so you better have something fresh. No more influencers."

"I know. I'd never bring you fluff. Your clientele wants a real slice of celebrity, right?"

"Yes. You've got excellent instincts, but you had that bad run last year. I was getting worried. You kept bringing in all those novelists."

"It was a phase. I thought reading might come back in.

But today I have something really special and I'm giving you first crack at it but it's going to be expensive."

"How expensive?"

"Ten times my normal fee."

Jeanette always paid Mandico well; she paid for exclusivity. But ten times the price? She looked at him skeptically. "It would have to be Jesus or Buddha for me to pay you ten times."

She only purchased DNA that nobody else had. Mandico knew Le Bouchon Elysian only served celebrities (famous and infamous) to her starstruck customers. The restaurant had its own growing vats in the basement, capable of producing up to thirty different meats. All they needed was a tiny sample of DNA and they could identify the tastiest cuts from any organism. Jeanette's chef was the renowned Sally Soyer, a culinary artist with two PhDs, one in molecular genetics and the other in philosophy. (The latter's dissertation was on the amoral nature of aesthetic choices.)

Most restaurants stuck to the in-vitro foods recommended by the FDA, but there were gray areas. The legislation was vague: As long as companies followed production guidelines, anything was acceptable. But most big food companies were only willing to produce conventional meat in-vitro: pork, beef, lamb, fish and, of course, chicken. It was rumored one company was working on ways to make everything taste like chicken. But a few bold foodies had stretched those boundaries leading to the popularity of the Endangered Biscuit Parlor, the Freaky Feed, and Pop-Ulars. The latter was a fast-food emporium which purported to sell the "most addictive food ever." The recipe was a trade secret, though after her analysis Sally had confirmed it was a mix of shrimp and the active components of the poppy plant.

"What could possibly be worth ten times our usual fee? You didn't kill someone to get the sample did you? Because I will turn you in, Mandico."

His head wobbled even faster. "Of course not. But I'm not sure you'll believe me. Tell you what. What if we let Sally run the analysis, and you buy me a drink?"

"You're a pirate, you know that, Mandico? If that's even your real name."

"Of course it's not. Now, how about that drink?"

Jeanette wanted to see if he could sip anything without spilling it. She nodded and took him to the kitchen.

Jeanette had inherited Le Bouchon Elysian from her father, a famous chef from France. Under his hand, it had been a well-respected restaurant focused on meat—a *bouchon* like the ones in his hometown of Lyons, but for all his fame as a chef it had not been popular. Eating animals had gained some of the social stigma of other vices. With the invention of in-vitro meat, the consumption of flesh no longer contributed to climate change, or to the brutally short life and death of countless animals sacrificed on the altar of human gluttony. Jeanette was among the first to realize that if you could grow beef in a vat, crassly called beaker beef by wags in the media, then why not human? Surely there would be an interest in trying all kinds of taboo meats, now that they no longer came from once-living animals.

It was a leap, but once she'd made it, Jeanette had the inspiration to serve only celebrities. Some of their dishes were determined by popularity—until recently, everyone wanted to try eating Hitler at least once—but some depended on Mandico's ability to procure DNA and the chef's ability to do something with it.

Sally had finished supervising that evening's rush and was

taking her customary drink afterward while the rest of the kitchen brigade cleaned up.

"Can you do a quick check on this for me? Mandico says you'll flip over it," Jeanette asked her Chef de Cuisine.

Sally's eyes lit up. She appreciated the buyer's nose for quality DNA as much as Jeanette appreciated his instincts for the market. She took the vial and went into her lab. "Back in ten." She spoke to one of her staff: "Alain, could you fix Madame Selavy and her guest a drink?"

"A cognac," Jeanette suggested. Normally she didn't spend much time in the kitchens, lab, or the *viandery*, the large room in their basement that housed the growing vats. She watched with pleasure while the *plongeur* and *marmiton* argued about baseball while cleaning dishes and pots. The kitchens, properly speaking, were Sally's domain, but everyone was deferential to Jeanette anyway.

"This is my last sale to you, by the by." Mandico's head bobbled some more in earnestness.

Fighting motion sickness, Jeanette asked, "And if I refuse?"

"I go straight to David's."

The drinks arrived and she toasted Mandico. She was thoughtful. "You could at least let me counteroffer. We've had a great relationship."

Mandico stopped moving, took a drink, and said, "Yes. But this is my last sale. And I'll need to disappear. You know, you could come with me."

Jeanette laughed, though she knew he was serious. If not for his nervous disposition and shady past, she might even have been tempted. He didn't take her laughter personally though, and raised his glass. They sipped companionably for a few minutes, watching Sally's kitchen staff do their thing.

Sally returned. She was clearly excited.

"It's unbelievable. It's not human."

"Oh," Jeanette said, disappointed. She couldn't believe that Mandico would scam her.

"It's not an animal either. Not an Earth animal, anyway."

"I'm sorry, what?"

"It's not any kind of biochemistry I've ever seen from DNA. It seems to have an extra base set in it."

"So what does that mean?"

"More interesting flavors, I hope. I've got the AI working on it. Don't worry, I'll be able to grow something interesting by tomorrow evening, and with any luck I'll have a way to serve it by Friday."

"Make it Saturday. And we'll put on a special evening. Perhaps we can get some media interest."

"Where did you get it?" Sally asked Mandico.

"Trade secrets. But they landed about a month ago."

"So you raided Area 51 or something?" Sally asked.

"Nothing so dramatic." Mandico sipped from his glass. "The aliens are staying at the Plaza. In Mick Jagger's old suite." He turned to Jeanette and said: "So, ten times?"

"Oh yes," Jeanette said, her head swimming with not only the fact that aliens existed and were staying at the Plaza, but the commercial possibilities of serving them with a nice sauce. "That's practically a steal."

"I know, but you've been good to me. Bonne chance," he said. "Wire it to the usual account."

The police visited the restaurant Friday morning. A haggard-looking Detective Johnson introduced himself and asked to speak with Jeanette in her office "privately."

Mandico had been killed. Quite expertly as it turned out, and Jeanette was one of his few known associates—and the only one who was legitimate, the detective pointed out not-so-subtly.

Jeanette was not easily frightened. In their second year of serving famous humans, Mandico had acquired the DNA of the late Queen of England, Elizabeth Windsor. Her rump was delicious grilled and served with a chutney of tropical fruits and was still a popular item on the menu. Though not as popular as the Anthony Hopkins with Fava Beans. However, the royal family did not take kindly to having one of their number served up to commoners. They sued— Jeanette won. When that failed to shut her down, two large gentlemen had tried to kidnap her, presumably to bring her back to the UK so she could be prosecuted there under the EU "genetic foods" legislation. But luckily her sommelier intervened. (In addition to having a wonderful palate and a vast knowledge of wines, he was an accomplished martial artist.) She'd brought in security measures thereafter.

"Do you know who did it?" she asked.

"We do not. Did he have enemies?"

"Only every celebrity whose DNA he acquired. I've served most of them too."

"Yes, that's quite a long list, isn't it?"

"My accountant should be able to supply you with a list of all the famous and infamous he's brought here." She shrugged.

"And where were you between the hours of eight and eleven last night?"

"Why, here of course."

"And you have witnesses."

"Many. Now is there anything I can actually help you with, officer?"

"Detective. No, thank you for your time."

When he left, she doubled security, and then, thinking she should be cautious, had it quadrupled. She wondered if perhaps the aliens had killed him. But that seemed unlikely after she watched the alien visit to the United Nations. It was all over the news.

Sally was pretty blasé about it, though. "By the way, I've found a steak that will blow your mind."

"You've already found a cut?"

"Sure. We don't have to grow the whole thing to test anymore. The software can extrapolate."

"And?"

"Delicious, though according to the AI it won't be as delicate as I'd like. The spectrometry reveals flesh that's a bit gamey, like venison, but it should have the sweetness of human too. It will be a crowd pleaser, I think, grilled with a reduced cherry sauce. Maybe something more exotic."

"What could be more exotic than alien?"

"You know," Sally said, "you're totally right. What's the point? I'll use cranberry in the reduction and that will be it."

The world was on fire with the aliens. They were epic. They'd carved out an asteroid and fitted it with engines, and spent the last one hundred years hurtling through space toward the far side of the galaxy. Turned out Earth was on the way. About eighty years into their mission they happened to catch some terrestrial radio broadcasts, and changed the trajectory of their mission to stop and say hi. They considered it a lucky break. Their spaceship was now a second moon orbiting the Earth.

They looked like purple versions of your average human, except they had four arms, pointy heads, and the men had functional mammary glands. The Soombarians, as they called themselves, were far more advanced and civilized than humans. They were so excited to meet another sapient species. At first.

In the United States, the President declared the day the aliens made contact a national holiday. Many other countries did the same.

The Soombarians planned to begin the exchange of cultural information the Saturday night following their arrival. Their Tansdarda would speak to the assembly of the UN and describe what it was like to live on Soombar; what the people of their world believed and hoped for and dreamed of. Tansdarda didn't mean leader. The honorific did not have a translation in any human tongue; the Tansdarda explained that he represented the focussing mind of the Soombarian's shared consciousness, and that a Tansdarda was only created on occasions when needed. The Tansdarda stepped up to the podium as each and every human being and Soombarian basked in the glory of their cosmic meet cute. Two vastly separated intelligences about to have intercourse, so to speak, for the first time. He stood before the podium and spoke in English. (They'd been learning it from more than twenty years of broadcasts.)

"We have come across the galaxy to meet you, our brethren, our brothers and sisters in consciousness. We are humbled by this. Humbled and glad."

Seconds earlier Sally supervised taking the faux alien

meat out of the stainless steel vats. Her *coupeurs* took the cuts of thick, almost purplish flesh up to the kitchen and threw them on the grill. The smell was intoxicating.

At this point, the Tansdarda began to scream. The Soombarians had an impressive lung capacity; except for a few gasping breaths, the Tansdarda screamed for nearly four minutes—two minutes for each side of the steak. When the Tansdarda finally stopped, he panted and said, "Somewhere nearby a Soombarian just died."

The assembly of humans erupted in outrage. Who would kill one of these beloved aliens, just as they were about to reveal their secrets? Who would be so stupid?

The Soombar-steaks were plated, sauced, and ready to serve when Jeanette addressed her most privileged clientele. They all knew they were there to taste alien. "This is something special. You will never experience this again. For the first time, humans will eat a cuisine, not of this Earth, but of another world."

Everyone applauded as they toasted Jeanette, and the waiters brought in the plates of food—a slice of alien with cranberry sauce, plus the day's best greens and frites.

The Tansdarda had recovered from the grilling and managed to return to his speech. He explained to the inhabitants of Earth how the Soombarians as a people had overcome the need to kill. First, they discovered peaceful ways of solving disputes, and found ways not to slaughter one another. They extended this pacifism to animals, and eventually, to plants. They learned to connect their consciousnesses. They drew nourishment from the universe itself. The average Soombarian was as ethical as Buddha or Jesus.

Just as the Tansdarda finished expressing his admiration for the Buddha's Eight-Fold Path and Christ's Sermon on the

Mount, he shrieked again, this time a cry of existential anguish that could only be described as disturbing.

The cry coincided with the instant the first of one hundred people who could afford to buy the most exclusive meal on the planet bit into their first taste of Soombarian. This happened to be Ronald Clump, the magnificently toupéd toxic narcissist who had produced a dozen skyscrapers and many other god-awful developments in New York; he chomped down on his "alien steak with fruit sauce," as he called it. Clump was a fine example of the class of humans destroying the planet.

At that moment, his sins flooded in on the Tansdarda. For Clump, it worked a little more subtly. He felt "funny." He felt like he was "wrong." With that first bite he understood that he was a gigantic asshole and felt badly about it. For the first time in his adult life, he felt shame. So much so that he left the table and called his assistant. He had a long list of people who needed to be paid, those he should rehire, and some who would need more serious amends.

Ninety-four other people in the restaurant had a similar experience. At the same time, the sins of all ninety-five hammered into the aliens' consciousness.

Five clients, on the other hand, felt the most wonderful well-being, harmony and belonging they'd ever experienced in their lives. They felt complete. Their love was justified. And if it hadn't been for those five, humanity would never have had the opportunities the Soombarians presented. The five were compassionate souls, and the Soombarians felt that much more strongly than they did the sins of the ninety-five.

The Soombarians were fully enlightened beings, aware of the other dimensions that some might consider spiritual, that connected them telepathically; and this consciousness extended to their genetic material, which acted as both a transmitter and receiver. But the Soombarians weren't quite down with the idea of being eaten by humans, though they could see how that could be beneficial. For the humans, at least.

———

Jeanette hadn't ever thought she'd meet an alien, let alone one she'd served her clients.

"So, we will leave you with our genetic material," the tall, purple, multi-armed Tansdarda told her. "But we beg you not to touch it until we've left orbit."

That was the agreement. They would provide DNA to the Earth, and, in turn, humans would refrain from eating them while the Soombarians could feel it. The sensation of being consumed was just too disturbing, even for a species as evolved as the Soombarians.

"So who killed Mandico?" Jeanette asked.

"Not us. If we'd known, we would have destroyed his samples. You know he sold to more than you, right?"

"That bastard!"

"You can hardly be angry with him if he's dead."

"I still am actually."

"That is hard to understand," the Tansdarda said. "But then, you are a human. And your emotions are primitive to us. Perhaps one of your competitors discovered his ruse and killed him for it."

"That may be," Jeanette said, thinking of the sketchy characters she knew Mandico had dealt with regularly. "In fact, it's probably likely. Even so, I *am* sorry about serving you to my clientele. If I'd known you were able to experience being cooked because of your advanced consciousness, I never would have."

"It only happens when we're close by," the Tansdarda reassured her. "Though even after we're gone our racial memories and ethos should still transmit to you through our flesh. But yes, the feeling of being cooked, even by a chef as talented as Sally, was unpleasant. I trust you'll wait until we're gone until you serve us again."

"Don't worry," Jeanette said. "We won't ring the dinner bell until after you've left orbit."

"Ah. I get that." The Tansdarda laughed and then was quiet for a moment. "When you've had a chance to absorb our wisdom, I hope our cultures can meet once again. You humans are very creative. Creative, but extremely dangerous. And a little too obsessed with celebrity, if you don't mind me saying."

Jeanette shrugged. "It's all a matter of taste."

6

THE HEIGHT OF ARTIFICE

THE WORST FORM of nostalgia is unrequited love.

Even so, the sun played on her blonde hair as I smiled at her from the street. I could have cast my eyes somewhere else, but some instinct told me this was the last image I'd have of her, so I watched. What I felt was not agony, but worse. It was an intense blast of bittersweet longing for that perfect day we'd never shared. She was wearing a buff leather coat with fringes on it. She smiled at an elderly man having some trouble getting on the tram, and she helped him to his seat. She looked glamorous while being so beautifully human. Superstar cool. Her hair glowed like a talisman I'd never again witness, reminding me not of what we'd lost, but of what we'd never had. Then the electrics kicked in, and she was gone.

Ding ding!

"We'll always remember this," she had said, the moment I'd met her. She was taller than me by a few inches, her skin perfect and teeth white like a celebrity's.

"What do you mean?"

"This was the moment we created your play."

I wasn't sure if she was talking to me, the play's writer, or to the director, Anne, who had arranged the meeting and would bring the production to life. In any case, I didn't care. I totally agreed. We weren't going to forget it. She was going to be the protagonist and with her in place, the play was sure to be a success. We needed a male lead, but surely, anyone could play that part?

She sat down. We were meeting in an art nouvelle café that had somehow survived the Dictatorship of the Proletariat. The waitstaff wore black and white and they took their jobs seriously. They were not only respected, but respectable. It was just after the Velvet Revolution so the choices on the menu hadn't caught up with Western Europe yet. It was terrifying how quickly that would change. But at that moment, it was five pm and we all just ordered pilsners.

"This is our Victoria," Anne said in a musical English accent.

I shook the actor's hand and she said, "I love your writing."

"Thanks."

"It's so insightful," she said. "You write women so well."

This was the first time I'd heard that compliment. "What makes you say that?"

"Oh, Victoria is just so real. It's like you've tapped into my mind."

Swooning is an underused word. It seems old fashioned and goofy, but that is what happened, as I momentarily phased out of reality. These were the words I dreamed I'd hear. I understood the human condition and, more than that, I'd expressed it in a way that other people could understand! And this glamorous American actor was telling me so.

Then she turned to the director, Anne, and asked: "How are you?"

They chatted for a while and I just sat there, enjoying the sound of her speech. She was clearly an alto, and her voice had a brogue I hadn't encountered before, which I now know is a Northern California accent. A bit strong, a bit staccato at times, but she could also mimic other accents when she wanted. A trait we shared. We loved imitating our British colleagues in the theatre group.

Anne left us. But my new lead actress and I stayed to discuss her part. She wanted to know if it was based on a real person. Her questions were detailed. Exhaustive. Eventually, I told her the entire character was a fabrication, based on my own imaginings. How I managed—as a man—to perfectly capture what she herself faced was a mystery; she wanted to know how I'd done it.

"Honestly, it was instinct," I said.

She nodded, the light in her eyes dimmed, and the conversation moved on to quotidian issues. Where we were living. How we were getting on with learning Czech. (Not well, in my case.) We discussed how hard it was to find fresh vegetables. And tooth floss. As the two North Americans in the theatre group, we often joked about our obsession with dental hygiene.

We saw one another regularly after that, even after she decided to drop out of the play. She had work conflicts, but I suspected the part was too revealing for her. I was disappointed at the time, but ecstatic that she still wanted to see

me. Our friendship grew. We had both been trained as jour-
nalists. She was quite a good one, working for an American
business publication in the city. I was earning my keep by
doing a radio column for the English-speaking service of the
Czech public broadcaster. She sang regularly at coffee shops,
accompanying herself on guitar. It seemed to me that she
could do anything she wanted. Every time she took to the
stage, she was luminous. I didn't miss a performance. She
was in a friend's play, and though my own had been a great
success, I wondered how much better it might have been had
she stayed on in the lead role.

She clearly had some kind of affection for me but that's as
far as it went. It never became physical, despite my overtures.
I just wanted to be around her. I hoped that eventually, she
would return my feelings.

I thought it almost happened one night at dinner. She had
joined me and a friend who were visiting the city. We talked
about my script, the part she had never played in the
production.

"He still won't tell me how he understands me so well,"
she'd said.

"Maybe he doesn't," my friend replied.

"Or maybe I just tapped into the universe, and it chan-
neled you to me," I suggested. "That could be it."

The look in her eyes was thoughtful, but distant.

And then we didn't see each other for some time. This
was back before the advent of the smartphone, or even
mobile phones. Most of us expats didn't even have landlines.
There was no way to check in on a friend, short of visiting
their flat or place of work; if you knew either. I found myself
frequenting all the places where I knew she liked to go. I

even asked about her at the café where she most frequently played guitar.

"That's right. I haven't seen her for a while," the bartender said. "Maybe she left town?"

The thought hadn't occurred to me. As soon as he said it, horror filled me. It happened all the time. "Prague is over," people would say, "I'm going to Budapest." Or Tallin, or wherever the hip set had determined was the "it" place to be.

Then from another regular performer at the cafe, I learned that she had started dating some Czech doofus named Jirka, who worked with her as a fixer. I'd met him. I didn't get it. They had almost nothing in common. He was kind of weird looking. Tall and gangly. What my British expat friends might call "a stick bug."

I was hurt. But I was old enough to have learned that attraction doesn't always go both ways. She admired my work, but she didn't fancy me, as Anne would say.

Yet... she seemed to indicate the opposite sometimes. The way she looked at me, as though waiting for the moment to be right. For the pieces of the puzzle to finally fit. After the hiatus—what I now realize was the start of her relationship with Jirka—we'd run into one another periodically. Not nearly enough.

Meeting in person was a kind of miracle. Without phones, you'd have to arrange your get-together ahead of time. Where and when. Then you'd both have to remember it and show up. These meetings became more infrequent than at the start of our friendship. More painful. But we ran in the same circles. And we'd chat. She'd say, "Let's get together." Love demanded that I turn up.

The last time we met was at a little coffee shop I liked. When I'd first arrived in Prague, I'd spend an hour walking there from my accommodations in Smichov, nurse a Turkish coffee for several hours while I read the paper and scribbled in my journal, and then walk back to my flat. Lonely times, but still, good. I'm not sure why I suggested the place. I got there first, as I often did those days. I had an ironic horror of being late, of leaving people waiting, mostly because I hated it so much myself. This meant I was always early, and it seems I spent half of my time in Prague anxiously lingering. I learned to suggest cafes and bars so I had a place to sit and something to do while I waited. I always had a book or my notepad with me so I could avoid the nonexistent stares of people wondering why I was on my own.

It's a form of raw ennui that we've lost. Again, because of the phones. Distraction and social distance are always on hand. But not then, so when she showed up, I was grateful. As always, I felt light-headed around her.

"How are you?"

"Great. Things with Jirka are fabulous."

"Uh. Great. How so?"

"Oh, he's just so sweet. Especially for a Czech man."

"Are you going to do any more acting?"

"No, I think I'm putting that behind me," she said.

"But you're so good."

"Thank you, but it's too hard."

"I get that." I was in the middle of writing my second play. It wasn't going well. The short stories I'd written were all being rejected. I'd even begun a novel, and I wondered some days if there was any point to writing anything. And that was just the written word. Actors, it seemed to me, had to be much stronger to go on in the face of their denials.

"Do you?" she said. Her eyes were wide with anticipation. Of what, I didn't know.

"Yes. The uncertainty of it. The rejection."

"That's not it. At all. It's not the rejection that bothers me. That's normal. Every director has their own ideas about who a character should be, and sometimes, you just don't fit. No, it's the lying."

I laughed.

"What?"

"What lying?" I asked. "You're joking, right?"

"No. That's what acting is. It's deception, from beginning to end. I'm sick of it."

"But..." I didn't know what to say. "Good theater, any art, reveals the truth. In a way that journalism can't."

"I'm tired of pretending. There's no magic to it," she said. "It's all artifice. You should understand that, more than anyone else." She looked at me with tears in her eyes.

"Why me?"

"Because... well, you imagined it. You wrote it."

I felt lost. She was crying now. Gentle tears, but no sobs or even a quavering voice. Just a few tears flowing down her cheeks.

"I'm... sorry?"

"It's okay. I knew it was too much to hope for. But it really was just all in your head, wasn't it?"

"What?"

"Your play. The lead, Victoria. You imagined her."

"Yes," I said. I still didn't understand.

"But you didn't know her."

"She's not real," I said.

"But she is. Was." She paused: "I'm not sure now."

For the longest time, I would look back, with terrible

cruelty, convinced there was still a chance. The love that I had for her could still have blossomed into something mutual, if I had been able to see the answer to the riddle she posed in that moment. But I didn't. I couldn't make the connection. We sat awkwardly in that silence. She wiped the tears from her cheeks.

"Well, I must get going."

I could feel my face burning. I felt nauseated, choking on the moment. I couldn't think of anything to say. I stood. As she put on her coat I said, desperately, "I'll walk you to the tram."

She smiled. "That would be nice."

I longed to reach out, to hold her hand, just for one second, but I knew that would be the wrong thing to do. It was all I knew, with panic. It was a gloriously sunny October day as we wound our way through the old streets of the Golden City. So beautiful. So romantic. A travesty. There was still a possibility, I could sense with a persistent and painful clarity. If I had found the words. But I couldn't because I didn't understand. Instead, we walked in silence as I tried to work out what was happening.

Ding ding.

The tram pulled away. She disappeared from my life forever. For many years, I was haunted by what I'd never understood. What she needed me to know about her. Yet it remained an enigma.

Unrequited love is the worst form of nostalgia. These days, I comfort myself with the thought that perhaps the mystery was much more easily solved:

I was just too short for her.

7

THE INFINITY EFFECT

PHYSICS HAD long since proved that the universe was finite. It *looked* infinite because of its topology but the concept of infinity was merely a human construct. Stodek was sure this was the key to his eventual escape.

He was locked in the United System's complex of infinity boxes at LaGrange Point Five. Each war criminal got his own box which, to the occupant, had no edges and no end. He, like the others, floated in the illusion of infinity.

All of Stodek's colleagues had gone mad. Eventually, their psychopathological behaviors had been crushed along with their egos, leaving nothing but gibbering, drooling, mindless husks. Sometimes, it took a very long time for the infinity effect, as the United System psychologists called it, to take hold. Stodek had been floating for years, and he had yet to crack.

"They will not take my great achievements away from me," he had said when they first put him into his infinite cage. But over the years, that statement had become more of a mantra— "my great, my great, my great, my great…"

He clung to his people's history like a lifeline. They had migrated to Ganymede in the early years of the solar system's colonization. Many had died. They had built the colony's infrastructure with the blood of their brothers and sisters, yet this did not matter in the eyes of the rulers of the United System hegemony—Stodek had never been able to bring himself to call it a government. The hegemony was more like a cancer—a riotous growth of corporate interests and commercialized culture that fed on a docile, racially mongrelized mass. The hegemony wanted Ganymede subservient to its laws and so-called culture, but his people had resisted.

A few other colonies had tried to maintain their independence. The Japanese on Io. The Teutonic Confederacy on Titan. Even the far-flung Gaels on the icy moon of Oberon had tried to maintain their cultural independence, though not with the same vigour as the others. No Gaelic leaders had been imprisoned in an infinity box when they'd been defeated. For Stodek's people though, there were many boxes, he noted bitterly. But he had no regrets. He knew that he would survive. "My great. My great."

The war had been brutal. Initially, Stodek and his troops had been successful. They'd destroyed the enemy throughout the Jupiter system. Then he and his soldiers had systematically shattered the enemy's morale. None of the other moons could resist his will—the will of his people to be free. But then the hegemony's fleet arrived and it was all over. His soldiers outnumbered. His ships destroyed. They'd had no choice but to surrender. Stodek and the other leaders were tried for their supposed crimes: the hegemony said they'd murdered, they'd raped, they'd done both in Stodek's name on a mass scale. Genocide, many times over. He was evil, as defined by the United System's Human Code of Ethics.

He laughed at that. Ethics. The United System hegemony claimed to be ethical, yet they did not allow his people, the brave citizen-soldiers of Ganymede, the basic human right of self-determination. The thought brought a tear to his eye and Stodek felt a stab of despair as he gazed at the grayness of infinity all around him.

He woke with a start. He had no idea how long he had been asleep. It might have been a minute or a month. Before sleep, he remembered vaguely, he had been screaming. He couldn't remember what he'd been doing before the screaming. He couldn't remember much anymore, and that worried him.

A man stood before him. He wore a tight black skinsuit, the mark of a court-appointed advocate. The man had a strange, blank look on his face, and except for a pair of ancient spectacles, he was unremarkable.

"Stodek," the advocate said in a soft, level voice.

"My great," Stodek answered.

"Eventually, you'll forget you're going to die. When that happens it won't be much longer until you lose all sense of individuality. The psychologists say that a new person, a good person, can then be applied to your physical shell."

"Lies!" Stodek screamed at the advocate. Life returned to him in a flash, and he remembered the first man he'd killed. The soldier's pressure suit had ripped and his blood had boiled away. Stodek smiled.

"They've let me come in to ensure that your human rights are not being violated," the advocate said without a hint of irony.

Stodek cackled. "My great, my great. They will not defeat

me, dog! I am Stodek! I am the leader. My people will need me. When I escape, I will lead them to—"

"To where? Out there?" the advocate asked, pointing into the hideous, endless gray.

Stodek moaned.

"You know, there are critics who say these infinity boxes are too cruel. They could instead wipe your mind with chemicals or nano. There are electronic methods. The critics say we should use those to reform you, Stodek."

"Never. My great."

"But the infinity boxes are not just about rehabilitation. You know that, don't you, Stodek? Did you know that the United System makes every 18-year-old spend one half-hour in a box? The same day they receive their voting franchise. Nowadays, everyone knows how horrible it is to be suspended in infinity. Oh, it seems cruel, but it is effective. We have virtually no crime."

"No. Crime." Stodek grinned. "There was no crime on Ganymede."

"Ah, I beg to differ," the advocate said. "There was no individual crime. There were plenty of state-sanctioned crimes. Think of the other groups that you deported. Or worse, left in the vacuum to die."

"Lies. Lies," Stodek answered. "My great. My great. My great. They polluted us with their presence. They had to leave. You will not torment me. You're reminding me of my great, great, great..." The word came slowly to Stodek but it came: "—achievements. My great achievements!"

Stodek felt a thrill of victory. The word "achievements" had been lost to him for some time. He would outlast their torture!

The advocate looked around uncomfortably. "This

unbounded space is nasty. The only thing that makes it bearable is knowing they're going to let me out soon. Do you know that war crimes have dropped to almost nil?" Stodek stared at him balefully. The advocate continued. "I say almost nil. It seems the human capacity for evil is infinite too."

It was an admission of defeat. He would survive to fight again!

"Of course," the advocate said reasonably, "you realize that I'm not actually here. I'm a product of your disintegrating mind, which is filling in the space, so to speak. You're reaching the end, Stodek."

"No! Lies. My great achievement!" Stodek raged. "My. Great. Achievement."

"If that's true, then perhaps you can tell me your first name?" The advocate winked at him and disappeared. The impertinent question lingered in Stodek's mind.

"My great. My. My. Name?" He did not know it.

Into infinity the man howled.

8

CLOSE TO THE WIND

THE LAST THING I remember is the walls of my apartment in Piraeus fading to a bleached outline... The slow pulsing of my arteries from life to something approaching death. It was a terrible moment, suspended within the aching I felt for Linda. The life that we had lost.

As I awake, I don't have a feeling of hope. I don't feel anything, which is odd because I sank into the void in a wash of emotion.

I am in a small cubical cell, no more than five or six paces a side. There is no furniture, no smell. No sound. It is devoid of color, everything a uniform white. Despite this, it is not bright, nor is it hard to see. I think it's the lack of sound that's most disturbing.

"Hello?" I say. There is no reverberation. It's as though I'm in a dead room. I walk to the walls to see if this is so, but they are plain and don't seem made of sound-absorbing materials.

"Is anyone there?"

Wait. There is a sound, like the background static you

might hear if you were listening to the universe with a radio telescope. I wait anxiously and realize that at least I am feeling anxiety. The whisper disappears, and I try to remember how I got to Piraeus, how they tracked me down there.

I can't remember. It's a horrible thing to accept. I can only recall a few things. Those last few terrible moments. The name Linda. The certainty that we had a beautiful life together, and that it was lost when I was put to sleep. Or whatever actually happened. A paltry handful of facts to base any course of action on.

"For God's sake. Is anyone there?" It's as though my voice didn't exist at all, the sound sucked into a vacuum. I do a quick circuit of the room and discover to my horror that there is no door of any kind in it. The low, sub-audible sound is there again. I'm feeling it more than hearing it. At least that impression is substantial. Everything else seems to be a mirage. Try. I must try to reconstruct what happened. There was the apartment. I know that. It was in Piraeus, the port just outside of Athens. Did I get there by ship? What was in the room?

Nothing.

A crashing wave of sound washes over me. It sounds like feedback, and it hurts, but I feel something else: Relief.

"Sam?" a digitized voice says to me. I can't tell if it's male or female, young or old, but it is a cure for my anxiety.

That's it. That's my name. Sam!

"Yes. Yes. Who is this? Is this Linda?"

The voice doesn't return for a moment. "Sam?"

"Yes. Yes. My name is Sam. Where am I?"

I wait for the reply. An agony of time passes. Finally, the

voice says, "It's hard to explain. Can you tell me what you remember?"

"Ah, no! I don't recall much. There was an apartment. In Greece. I think it was the port of Piraeus. There was a woman named Linda. I was... drugged, I think is the best way to describe it. Can you help me?"

I wait for a reply again. The voice is a lifeline, but a tenuous one, as if they're speaking to me from across the solar system.

"Yes, Sam. We're here to help you. You're going to have to stay here for the time being, but we plan to get you out. Can we get you anything?"

"Information. Please! How long have I been out? What year is it? Can you tell me about Linda?"

I'm getting used to the lag time now, and eventually the response comes, in a flurry of information that cascades over me like a heavy roller in the deep ocean. "Linda died nearly a century ago. You've been sequestered for many, many years in a kind of... stasis. The world is a different place now, Sam, and it's not going to be easy for you but if you're willing to be patient I can guarantee you that you'll have the opportunity to explore it again. On our terms. Is that clear?"

It's clear. Linda is dead. She's gone.

I'm surprised, again; there is no despair at this thought. Sadness, yes, but not the anguish I remember. It occurs to me that there's something ominous in the voice's tone. I don't like the sound of "our terms." The changed world should be no problem because I don't recall the way it used to be, but something tells me not to say that. I phrase the next question succinctly: "Am I a prisoner?"

The delay is even longer this time. Finally, the voice

responds: "In a sense, yes. You may not recall this, but you used to be an extremely dangerous individual."

A likely story. I don't feel like a dangerous individual. I'm hardly an individual at all, given how little I know of myself. But something within me tells me that these people are not my friends, though they claim they're going to help me. I'd better play along with them, lest they know my mind.

"I don't remember being dangerous. I can promise you that I won't hurt anyone if you let me out. But I'm willing to wait until you're sure."

Let them chew on that! This time the response comes quicker: "Thank you, Sam. We hoped you would take that attitude. It will all be so much easier that way. We're going to turn the lights out for a while so that you can have a sleep. Is that okay?"

"Oh, sure. As long as I wake up sooner this time."

They don't respond to my joke. The white cube disappears. I'm suspended in a void, but I'm not unconscious. I should be terrified. I'm not. Without the light, there is literally no sensation. Maybe they're right. Maybe I am dangerous. You're supposed to feel fear in a situation like this. And I'm not feeling much of anything. I'm even losing my connection with Linda. Dead a hundred years! I know now that once I loved her, but even that is gone. Faded like the apartment walls in Piraeus. They are diminishing in detail, leaving only the traces of old facts.

I walk a few paces, and do not meet the edge of the cube. I keep walking, and there is still no wall. My hands out in front of me, I keep moving, pushing forward against the absence of a barrier. Something tells me that my captors would not like my movement. My freedom.

I keep pressing into the void, looking for... something.

This seems to take a long time, though it's hard to be sure. Eventually, I hear the distinct sound of the ocean. Somewhere ahead is the tangy smell of salt water. I have an emotion I recognize: the desire to be free. To sail the oceans again, as I'm sure I did before…

———

Dr. Vermeer unplugged himself from the interface. He smiled at his colleague, Dr. Maquez. "We did it. He's still alive."

The scientists, both Fellows at the Institute for Consciousness Studies, had just made a breakthrough that would doubtless garner them both the Nobel Prize. Vermeer put the VI jack down on his desk and turned off the veridical interface—a device capable of creating a near perfect virtual representation of the world—before facing Maquez again. The headset had turned his white hair into a nest of cowlicks.

Though they had once been lovers, now Vermeer thought of Maquez in professional terms only. Maquez was twenty years younger than Vermeer, but looked like an undergrad fresh out of high school. She was one of a genetically select few for whom regeneration treatments actually reversed the aging process instead of merely forestalling it. It was one of the many reasons they were now only colleagues.

"Did it suspect what it was?" Maquez asked Vermeer, her Brazilian accent thickening in her excitement.

"Oh goodness, no," said Vermeer. "Though I think he was suspicious of our need to keep him confined."

"Nothing we can do about that," Maquez said, resisting an impulse to pat Vermeer's hair back into place. "We can't risk repeating what happened when it formed."

Vermeer nodded. Though neither of them had been alive at the time, the incident had been a legend in artificial consciousness research. An entire power grid taken over to feed it. A similar outcome now would be disastrous—millions could die—which was why the Institute had been so exacting in their safety protocols. The risks were great, but so were the potential rewards: The possibility of actually understanding the only true artificial consciousness ever to exist. By studying Sam, they believed they might learn how to recreate him. Though science had long promised it was right around the corner, the ability to create true artificial intelligence at will continued to elude humanity. Two hundred years after the advent of the microchip, it was still only a promise.

Only Sam, completely by accident, had managed to achieve sapience. Unfortunately, along with it he had somehow been able to recreate the entire world virtually, eating up memory and energy at an exponential rate.

"But I don't like deceiving him," Vermeer said. "He'll have to trust us for our experiments to be possible. Now, let's get the first set of—" He was interrupted by an abrupt power outage.

"What's that?" Maquez made no attempt to hide the fear in her voice.

Then they heard the siren.

The ocean is ahead of me. Of that I am certain. I have no idea how long I've been walking in the void. I hear the roar and sweep of the river ahead of me. I run toward the noise.

It's deafening. But the joy of having the palpable sound

wash over me! I still cannot see, but I can sense the might of the watercourse. There's no way around it, and part of me knows that the only way to get to the ocean is to immerse myself in this jet. I sense its power. There are no rapids, only the current.

This is the moment when I must decide. Return to my captors or take my chances in the river. I realize now that I have had this choice all through my long march in the darkness—I could always go back. To what? They are uncertainties. They want something from me, and they have held me prisoner. In stasis they called it. They kept me from Linda... my wife. She was my wife, and they kept me from her.

I decide on the river and leap into it.

It nearly destroys me. The strength of the current threatens to tear me apart. I roll into a ball, my chin in my chest, and let the river take me where it will. It's agony, but the longer I survive in the turbulence the slower it becomes. The pain lessens, and then the river is a stream, and I can uncurl my body. Then a brook, a trickle.

I can see again. There is light. I see the banks of the river slick with mud, but it's easy to climb up the sides. At the top I see high-rise buildings, black with armor plating, in many strange geometric shapes. If I could remember the world before, I'm sure that I would know this landscape is completely foreign to what it should be. The high-rises seem to be inhabited, so I make my way toward them. The ground is flat, hard, and reflective. Pulses of light occasionally shoot underneath me but soon they stop too. Everything behind me is quiet, while ahead the buildings seem to quiver in anticipation. They seem almost alive, menacing.

I reach the first building, a massive dodecahedron at least thirty stories high. The angle of the wall is above me, and I notice that it casts no shadow. The black of the armor plating absorbs all light. There is no reflection as my hand reaches toward it. The wall is cold, painful to the touch, but after the torment of the river it does not seem so bad. I push forward, the fingers of my hand tight together, knife-like, and I am rewarded with a tearing sound as my arm pushes into the black wall. Soon, my whole body is through.

The world begins to take on a familiar shape. It's an office building. There are many rooms. Furniture. Color and light that behaves as it should. People walk about their business as if it's just another day. They hardly seem to notice me. I want to go to them, to ask for their help, but who knows if they are involved or not?

Instead, I find an empty office, close the door, and turn on the computer that sits on the desk. I need data. First, I search for Linda. It seems ludicrous. All I have is her first name and mine: Sam. The knowledge that we were once married, and that she died nearly one hundred years ago. My fingers are a blur, and the information is there before me. Her face, so lovely. And biographical details. And my face. And more details.

Apparently, I died not long after Linda. The portrait of me is more detailed than Linda's. It says that I was the creator of the first sapient artificial intelligence. An intelligence that formed accidentally, that became a simulacrum of me, creating the world in a virtual way as it acquired conscious-ness. My head swims. How can I possibly be dead? I'm alive. In this room, typing on this computer. I can feel the plastic under my fingers, smell the slight staleness of the room. It's real. Perhaps this information was planted by my captors. Perhaps I discovered more that they intend to get from me. One thing is sure: If they lied about my death, then they could certainly have lied about Linda's death too. I can't ignore the possibility that she's still alive. According to her biography, the last place we both lived was in Ireland— I'm sure that I will find her there!

Outside the office door several uniformed guards are waiting for me. They move so slowly that I can walk by them before they can draw their revolvers. In a moment I'm past them and out the front door of the building.

The sky above is a deep cerulean blue. It reminds me of the ocean I must cross to get to Linda.

"We've lost it," sighed Maquez.

The last hour had been tortuous. Somehow the AI had remained conscious when they powered down the program heuristics and the artificial cell. Though the cell was not connected to the net, it had escaped.

Vermeer was still recovering from the shock. He sat in his chair with a slack look of disbelief on his face. "I can't believe we lost him."

"My God, Carl! Snap out of it. We have to explain this to the Institute. I was able to follow it through the power mains to the net cluster downtown. But I couldn't get a powerful enough containment program when I found out where it was." Maquez looked at her datapad again. "It accessed Linda and Sam Moriarity's biographical details. Why would it do that?"

"Do what?"

"Come on, Carl." Maquez got up from the veridical interface where she'd been tracking the AI and sat next to Vermeer. "Look. If we're going to salvage this situation I'm going to need your help. You're the psychologist. Why would it look at those files?"

There was no response. It was like old times: Maquez trying to say something really important and Vermeer ignoring her. She slapped him.

Vermeer looked up, his face hot with anger. "You haven't done that since—"

"Never mind that! Think about the problem. You're supposed to be a scientist! Why look at those biofiles?"

"He's trying to find Linda."

"How? She's dead."

"But what if he still thinks he's Sam Moriarity? The record of the original event is unclear, but some theorized that the AI entity transferred Moriarity's life to his own heuristic. I was thinking that it'd make a great paper, if it was true. Imagine. You're a scientist trying to create an artificial entity, and you think you failed. Then through some kind of... digital evolution he takes on your history. Think how much data about each of us is accessible. He could recreate you in the net, just like a VI."

Vermeer thought for a moment, drifting away, but then returned to his hypothesis. "Anyway, say he thinks he's Sam Moriarity. His bio would say that Moriarity's dead, and clearly, he's not. So the entity might reason that perhaps the bio is also lying about his wife being dead. That we lied."

"You mean *it*," said Maquez.

Vermeer looked at her questioningly.

"It. It. This thing is not a human being, so we say: it."

"Well, you can't deny *it* has a personality. This is our own fault for arrogantly assuming that we should have control over another—"

Maquez interrupted him with a heavy sigh. "Look, there's

no point debating the potential human rights of an artificial being. Especially if it starts using computing resources at an exponential rate like it did before."

Vermeer considered the scale of potential casualties. Everything relied on the network, from power grids to safety protocols on transport. Millions could die in the initial veridical cutoff and many would perish after. "How do we capture him?"

"God, I'm not even sure that we can track it."

Vermeer looked away. "Let's try to out-think him then. Where do you suppose he's going?"

She didn't bother to correct Vermeer's pronoun. "What do you mean, where? It's an artificial digital entity."

"But he doesn't know that. He's going to search for the local net that corresponds to the geographic location that he's trying to find. Think, Carmen. And do it quickly. Remember that he has the advantage of speed on his side. Our reaction times are a fraction of his."

Maquez looked at him, genuinely impressed. It could work. They could anticipate it.

They sat there thinking. Except for the hum of the veridical interface on standby, the lab was silent.

The air is filled with the roar of the wind as my ship hauls as close to it as I can. It's an unseasonable easterly, but I can use it to make good time. The roll and hiss of the waves is like a balm to me. I have definitely sailed before, and what better way to elude pursuit? There is no electronic or paper trail to follow, and the ocean is wide.

My days are filled with the sounds and smells of the sea.

The simplicity of it is beautiful. Sky. Sea. Waves. Wind. The only alien features of the scene are the ship and me. A few days pass and soon I can smell the richness of earth. Before I can see land, I sense it and then the gulls find me. I have sailed close to the wind the whole way. But now I tack towards my destination. The dark shattered islands that make up the Blaskets. Dangerous waters for those unaware of the submerged rocks.

I make for Ballydavid Head, lying underneath the brooding mass of Mount Brandon. Who knows how long it's been, but I have finally returned to the Dingle Peninsula where Linda and I once had a cottage. Perhaps there I will find her, waiting for me to return.

―――――

"Yes. See," said Maquez.

Her eyes stared blankly in VI, but she spoke excitedly. "I've picked up a spike in the usage of the transatlantic routers. Some huge piece of data is slowly processing itself across the ocean. Could that be it?"

"He might sail. Moriarity was a sailor. And remember what he... it ... said about remembering a port? Is it making for Ireland?"

"Who knows? Why is it moving so slow?"

"My guess is the dataspike is the AI creating the reality of a sailing voyage," said Vermeer. "If only there was some way to know. Imagine the possibilities!"

"It would depend on how good it was at interpreting reality, but it could make us a fortune in the virtual nets."

"I meant the scientific possibilities." The computers chimed, and Vermeer asked, "What was that?"

"Something's changing. Yes. The dataspike is now in the Irish net. I'll dispatch our capture virus. I hope it works."

"God help us if it doesn't," Vermeer said.

I don't remember the cottage, but I know that I used to live there. It's like other buildings along the windswept coast. Single-story bungalows with bright whitewashed walls, and jaunty doors painted red or blue or bright green. Our place has a blue door, reminiscent of the sea that it faces. Instead of a traditional thatched roof we have a slate roof. There is a small satellite dish for internet access, as we are off the landlines on this remote part of the peninsula. Apart from knowing that it's ours, I have no other emotions about it. Again, I feel empty but deep within me is the knowledge that I did not always feel this way.

I knock on the door tentatively, and there's no answer. I look in the window and can see that there is a light on in the bedroom. The door is unlocked. I step in and close the door behind me.

"Linda?"

A voice answers from the bedroom. "Yes, hon? Where have you been? It's been days."

Something about her voice is wrong. It's comforting, but I don't know... I walk toward the light spilling from the bedroom door. She is there! I can see her lying on the bed reading a magazine. She is beautiful. My Linda. If only I could remember more, but suddenly the feeling starts to flow inside me. I love her. I do know that, though I could not tell you what love means or what it is really, except the closest thing to joy. I run into the room and lie down on the bed next to her. She looks up from her magazine and says, "What's wrong?"

"I've missed you. You don't know what's happened..." I struggle for words, and then I notice that her face isn't changing. It's blank, as if waiting for something. A cue. My feelings of joy turn cold, and then her hand snakes out to touch me.

A tremendous noise, a cacophony of electronic sounds fills the air, and suddenly I find myself frozen within her arms. Her head cocks slowly to one side, machine-like, and her voice sounds wrong, speaking with a strange accent as it says, "We'll keep you safe, Sam. Safe here."

I scream. The world explodes in light and fury.

A trickle of blood flowed from the veridical interface plugged behind Maquez's ear. Her eyes were blank, her neck bent to one side, her hands frozen in the posture of an embrace. Vermeer could tell right away that she was dying by the way the spark of intelligence faded from her eyes. He quickly checked her pulse and ordered the office AI to call in the emergency squad.

He wished he had attended the first-aid seminars at the Institute so that he could do something more for her. No doubt the paramedics would arrive in time for them to save her, assuming her brain wasn't fried. It had been decades since someone had died of veridical feedback. But he rallied from this shock and forced himself to turned back to his science. There was still a chance that he could reason with the intelligence.

His fingers shook as he unplugged the bloody VI from Maquez's socket and inserted it into his own jack.

Vermeer found himself standing on a windswept coastline. Before him he could see little more than a sleek, tall-masted sailboat and dark ocean. To the right he could see a hill, and perched on top of it, a crumbling Napoleon-era signal tower. To the left was an expanse of low cliffs topped with thick luxuriant grass that hissed and whispered in the strong ocean breeze. Below him was a little cove. A man was pulling a small dingy down to the ocean. He could smell the salt tang of the sea. Vermeer could not believe how real it felt. This was something new. As veridical reality had been a generational improvement over virtual reality, this was a quantum leap beyond. It was indistinguishable from the real world. He imagined the possibilities.

But the entity was getting away.

The man follows me from the cottage and appears on the shale beach just as I'm about to launch the dingy and get back on my ship.

"Wait!" he says.

"Wait for what? More people to capture me? I'm not going to let you put me in a cage again! I'm going to find her. The real Linda."

"But I wasn't lying to you before. She's dead."

"Oh yes. Just like me."

"No. You're different, Sam. A special case. That's why we

had you in that *cage* as you called it. We need to understand you so that we can help you."

"What's there to understand? I'm a man with partial amnesia. I can remember my name, that I used to love a woman, that I had a life... but there are no details about it. It's like my memory was wiped clean! So you tell me, Dr. Vermeer. What do I need to understand?"

He stands there thinking about something. He looks solemn, and for a moment—a brief moment—it almost seems like he's being honest with me.

"So how did you know my name then?"

"What?"

"How did you know my name? If you have amnesia."

"Perhaps I knew you as well. Apparently I can remember names."

"I have another explanation," Vermeer suggests immediately.

Something tells me not to listen to whatever it is he has to say. It's going to be horrible. I just know it. Without waiting for another word, I launch the dingy into the cold water, and begin rowing as hard as I can. But the wind plays one of its tricks and instead of ripping the words away from me, it carries them to me:

"You are not Sam Moriarity! You're an artificial..." The wind interferes again, and his words seem faint, unreal. Don't listen. Don't listen.

When I get to my ship, I can see that he's left the beach, and I know that I must move on, before they can find me.

I head south, into the wind again. The sail hauls close, and I can feel the ocean slipping underneath me. A mystery as deep as my own.

9

AFTER THE INTERNET

Professor Roger Chandra's hands never left the small keyscreen. He let his car and the London road system take care of the driving as he worked on lecture notes for his first-year class in media history. He barely noticed as his Honda zipped over the CanWest bridge to Western University. He entered the tunnel underneath University College hill to the Manulife Think Big parking complex. Unfortunately, his hands were not typing. Words failed him as he couldn't think of a way to describe what the world was like before the internet became pervasive.

At fifty-five, Chandra felt like an anachronism. For the last few years, he'd found the students taking his first-year course at the Faculty of Digital Arts and Sciences were unable to understand even the most basic concepts, such as "mass media." They were all convergence-era kids, having grown up in a world where separate forms of media—TV, radio, newspapers, websites—no longer existed. In their experience, information, entertainment, communications— everything—was interconnected and their sources were practically invisible. First on their phones, and then in their brains.

In his work, Chandra called it the datasphere. For his students, it was like gravity. Its pull was always there, and they couldn't escape it. For Chandra, explaining a world before the datasphere was like trying to explain the General Theory of Relativity to a fish. He could do it, but the fish wouldn't understand.

The quiet whir of the engine stopped and went silent. Chandra sat there, fingers still poised at his keyscreen. Still nothing came.

It was Thursday, October 25, 2036.

Chandra sighed and slipped the screen in his satchel, careful to ensure that it was hidden. He was marginally ashamed of the device, given that his area of expertise was digital culture. Most of his peers had taken to AI composition years before, and only a few Luddites insisted on actually using a keyboard for their work. Most of his undergrads didn't even know how.

His watch chimed to let him know he needed to look at it. He sighed again. It was a message from his Nike, his office assistant AI, letting him know a student was waiting.

Chandra had refused to have a permanent datalink surgically implanted in his brain to connect him to the datasphere. They were expensive, but it wasn't just the money that gave him pause. He didn't trust them. He could have used dataglasses–the device was almost as good as the implanted link as it projected information directly onto the retina. But he had a defect in his eyes that meant he couldn't wear them. Which left Chandra only his watch and his keyscreen to keep him connected when he was out of his office, car, or home, where there were screens and holos to keep him linked 24/7.

Concealed scanners in Chandra's office door identified the student visually and by the student's identicard signal. (All security systems used them; it was just too easy these days to fool facial recognition AI.) Jaron Leonard was a mature student in his fourth-year seminar, Web Browsers and Other Transitional Media of the Early 21st Century. This cheered Chandra up immediately. He found Leonard personable and intelligent and he enjoyed the young man's Caribbean accent. It was not the first he'd heard; there were many refugees from the intense hurricanes that scoured the islands each year. Plus, Leonard had one of the finest minds he'd taught in years.

The people-mover brought Chandra to the Coca-Cola wing of the New Middlesex Disney building, and he took the stairs up to his office.

"I consulted your schedule, Professor Chandra, and it said you would be stopping by your office, so I thought I'd take a chance. Can you meet with me for just a moment?"

"Certainly, come in," said Chandra as the scanners recognized his identicard. (Like his student, he was mandated by the university to carry one if he didn't have a datalink implant.) The door opened. Inside there was a desk, an office chair, a couple of comfortable reading chairs, and a small, archaic library. Very early 20th century Bauhaus.

They sat down and Chandra asked, "Now what can I do for you?"

"I'm here to ask you about a reference I came across while studying for the mid-term. Apart from a standard Wikipedia description I got from my Nike, I can't find a thing on it. What was "linotype?""

"Ah. Well, linotype was a kind of composer for newspapers. It produced lines of type in metal that they used to print the paper."

"But why metal?"

"For use on the press. It was really clever. I'll send you the references on the whole process." He said to his unseen Nike-branded AI: "Send Jaron Leonard my ten best references on 'linotype.' Just do it." The AI would do the search from Chandra's personal teaching files, collect the relevant articles and virtual reports from the datasphere, and send it to Leonard's student Nike AI.

"Thank you," Leonard said. "You know I couldn't find anything on it, sir."

"Sure. And please. Call me Roger. And this is exactly why I keep saying it's such a shame there isn't search software or library access provided for undergrads anymore. Those student Nikes are hopeless. Now, do you mind if I ask you a question?"

Leonard nodded, but he looked nervous.

"I believe you told the class that you grew up in Antigua, right? Did you have complete internet access when you were growing up?"

"Oh, no sir. Roger. When I was a boy, they were just starting to roll it out. In All Saint's we had to connect to the web on an ancient computer. It was much like you describe in the class holos. We had to go to a terminal, you know, just to get access. And then it was usually just two-dimensional viewing on a screen. Then Margot hit us, and we came to Canada."

Chandra remembered Hurricane Margot; it had killed thousands and destroyed huge swaths of the Leeward Isles, one of many killer storms.

"So you remember what it's like living without the datasphere?" Chandra asked.

"If you mean the net, being connected all the time in virtual, yes. Yes, I do, sir. Roger."

"How would you describe that?"

Leonard thought for a moment and said, "It was more imaginative. Now everything is presented to you on your glasses, or through your link. Everything is just... given to you."

Leonard was about to leave when he said, "You know. I think I miss those days."

"Me too, Jaron."

The student left Chandra sitting in his reading chair surrounded by his books. And the datasphere. It was all around him. Pulling on him like Earth's gravity. Except for deep space, there was nowhere Chandra could go without feeling either. He thought about that for a moment, and then finally had his answer. He contacted the building supervisor and asked, "Can I get my classroom disconnected?"

"I'm sorry, Professor Chandra?"

"I'd like to disconnect a room from the net entirely for at least one hour of my lecture."

The supervisor looked shocked. "I don't know, Professor. We could do it, of course. But we'll have to cut the power and the back-up systems. And then their implants will probably pick up a signal from the Weston wing. You'd need some kind of shielding, or a signal interceptor. Besides, I'm not sure how students would react. It might freak them out. Besides, why on Earth would you want to?"

Chandra smiled. "I need to explain the gravity of their situation."

10

HOUNDING MANNY

I'M up way past my bedtime, but it's no fun. Since Dad and I got to the moon I haven't been sleeping so much. I keep having the same dream: The one where Mom gets all eaten by the nanites. The experimental bugs that everyone likes but me.

And then there are the other bad dreams that really aren't dreams at all. In one, the mean kids—the Trongs—all chase me and beat me up, and then I kind of shift back to the really bad dream, where the bugs are eating me. When I finally get to sleep, that's usually when I hear Dad yelling out, and he wakes me up, and I lie there in the dark, listening to the sounds of the air pumps, the hum of machines, and I just have this terrible feeling inside that the morning is going to come, and then I'll have to go to school.

The lights come on slowly, like a winter dawn back in Metoronto. I hear Dad up and making breakfast, and I get up because he gets angry when he has to make me get ready for school.

I hate Luna One. It was supposed to be fun, but I hate it.

And I can't get Dad to understand. "Isn't it time for school?" he asks me as he tries to get his bloodshot eyes to read the morning newsplass. He doesn't notice that I'm not wearing my special suit. I hate that suit.

"Yeah."

"Well, better be off then. Don't want to make a bad impression by being late in your first week here." He's said that every morning since we arrived, and I guess it's true. I don't want everyone to think I'm some gormy Earth kid that doesn't even know what time it is. Maybe today will be different. Maybe they won't pick on me.

School's okay, but afterwards they're waiting for me outside Lock 12. The whole city is underground and filled with tunnels and corridors and passages and these *airlock* places. And just like yesterday, they're waiting for me.

They call themselves the Trongs. The leader of their gang is Jordan Alvarez. Jordan is a thirteen-year-old meany, the son of a pair of permanent colonists—lifers. Jordan is hanging upside down from the airlock by his toes, as if it is the easiest thing in the world. My teacher, Ms. Deach, says that gravity on the moon is less than a sixth of what it is on Earth, but I'm still impressed. At least, I'd be impressed if he wasn't such a jerk.

"Where ya scuttlin,' Earthworm?" Jordan taunts.

The other Trongs crowd behind him, their weird long bodies blocking the passage behind their upside-down leader.

Everyone is about my age, ten-and-a-half, except for Jordan and his brown-nose sidekick Curtis. He's almost as ugly as Jordan. They're only a year-and-a-half older, but they are *all* way taller than me, and Jordan's almost as tall as Dad. I think it's the only good thing about living here. It makes you tall fast. I'd kill to be that tall.

Jordan lets go of the door with his toes, falls easily to the floor, and flips forward with his hands.

To be that graceful.

All of these Trongs are moon kids, born and raised. Dad says they mass less, which is a fancy way of saying they're not as heavy. They've grown differently from me, in ways that give them longer, more lithe arms and legs, ways that give them every advantage and me none.

Jordan flashes a hand sign to the others. There are six of them today in addition to Curtis. They move in for the kill, chanting as they get closer: "Earth WORM, Earth WORM, Earth WORM." Its rhythm makes me hate them even more, and it even scares me a bit. You see, I got in a lot of fights back in Metoronto when Mom died, so Dad sent me to a special trainer. I know all these cool ways of defending myself, but they don't work so good here.

Until we landed on Luna, I'd never lost a fight after my training. And it ticks me off. All I have to do is land one good one and these spindly freaks would leave me alone. Just like what happened at home.

Jordan moves in first and this time I wait for him to attack before I react, 'cause that's how he always gets me. I get off balance real easy. But I do it again, and somehow the suck-face just pushes me enough to send me skittering backward. It feels like I'm falling down, so I jump ahead, sail through the air, and nearly brain myself on the airlock. I land just beyond the Trongs, but before I can catch my breath and run away, they are around me again.

The younger Trongs dance and jeer, swirling around me in a sea of bright primary-colored skinsuits. After the younger kids finish seeing who can get the most punches in on my arm or leg in one pass, Jordan moves in for the kill. Today the final attack is mercifully short. I'm so mad, but I'm totally wiped. Each time those scrawny kids dance by me, I try to strike at their solar plexuses, knees, whatever, just like I was taught. My balance is all off. I watch Jordan approach warily; the lunie moves with grace, but his face is a mishmash and ugly: nose too big, eyes too close together and a weak chin that disappears into his chicken neck. I try to play possum and hold up my hands.

"What's wrong Manfred?" Jordan cackles. "Worm-fed can't take it?"

The others, led by that nasty Curtis, who has a thin, reedy voice, join in on the call: "Worm-fed, Worm-fed!"

Jordan saunters closer, and I leap, timing it so that I'll hit Jordan in the chest. The sucking gravity messes it all up. I zoom over their heads again when Jordan slips to the side, slapping me on the face as I fly past. I'm all uncoordinated and I land hard, and everything fades out for a moment, though I can hear the slap slap of barefoot Trongs running away from me, the distant sound of scornful laughter.

"You're never going to learn are you, Wormy?" says a voice in the gloom.

The blackness fades and then I can focus and for a moment I figure it's another Trong stayed behind for one more slap. I can still feel the sting on my cheek. Instead, I realize it's a pretty red-haired girl with bright green eyes from my class. She's kneeling next to me. I don't cry. But I can feel it trying to get out. She looks away, real nice-like, and I pull it together.

"Come on, Wormy," she says softly. "Getting angry isn't going to help you."

"What will?" My eyes burn. "I can't even touch them. They just dance all around me."

"You have to learn, just like I did."

"Learn what?"

"How to do things here." The pretty girl sits beside me. "My name's Tina. My mom is the Chief Medical Officer," she adds proudly.

"So you're a lifer?"

"Yep. Been here two years now."

"So, you remember what it's like on Earth?"

"Oh yeah, but I like it here a lot more. Come on, get up. Remember. Gently."

Good thing she says it. I almost launch myself upright like the orbital plane Dad and I took to Kennedy Space Station. But Tina's hand holds me down. She is only a little taller than me, probably more because she's older.

"Thanks. My name's Manfred Acteon. But I like to be called Manny. That's what my mom used to call me." Her little Manny.

"Where is she?"

"Oh, she died. The nanobugs killed her. They say it was her own fault."

Tina is quiet for a moment. But she doesn't get that sucky sympathy look on her face. I like her. "My Daddy died when I was real little. I don't remember him. Come on. Let's go back to the school and then I'll show you another way home."

"But there isn't any other way!"

"Sure there is. Dumb Wormy."

"Don't call me Wormy."

"Okay. Dumb... Manny." She says it in a nice way, so I don't get mad. Besides, I kinda like the way she's still holding my hand.

We get back to the school where another group of kids are gathered. For a bad moment, I think it might be more

Trongs waiting for me, that they sent Tina to torment me again. But they look a little different from the Trongs. They all have skinsuits, but their colors are different—lots of different colors. More fun. Most of the kids are shorter too, with bigger muscles.

"These are the Drins," Tina explains. "They're my friends, and if you can learn how to live on Luna One and help us, they can be your friends too."

The tallest of them comes forward and puts her fist on my shoulder. Weird. Like some kind of gang thing from home. She is real pretty, and I'd say she's about three years older than me. Her teeth almost shine from a light brown face, just like a girl I knew in Metoronto who came from Brazil. It's an easy smile to like, and her brown eyes kind of sparkle.

"I'm Jess. If you can pass the tests, then you'll be a Drin. Tina will be your initiator." With that, the smile disappears and the other Drins, all of them, turn their backs on me.

As Tina takes me away, I say, "That was weird."

"That's how we do it. We have to look out for one another and we make sure that everyone can pull their weight when they're here. Especially someone like you, Dumanny." She grins.

"What's that mean?"

"That's your name isn't it? Dumanny?"

"Just Manny! Besides, I'm not staying in this stupid city forever."

My dad is a nanotechnology architect. He and mom used to work together, until she died. Then he brought us to Luna One. It's just for a year. He says that's about as long as the human body can live in the reduced gravity of the moon without having permanent changes, like the stuff that's happened to the Trongs. A year seems like forever, but at least I know I'll be able to go back to the Earth.

"It's not stupid. Here, I'll show you."

Tina takes me up a hidden ladder about three corridors away from Lock 12. At the top of the ladder is an access tube. She takes out a cool power multitool and unlatches the opening to the tube. "After you," she says, and I crawl into the tube. It seems cramped, but it's wide enough for us to crawl along side-by-side. Tina shows me how to close the hatch after we're in the tube. There's a magnetic thingy that lets you do it so that it's closed from the corridor.

While we crawl along, Tina explains, "You'll have to change the access tunnels you use from day-to-day, 'cause the Trongs will figure out that you're using these to avoid them. But there aren't too many Trongs, so you should be able to do it. Besides, in here you're going to have the advantage."

"Why's that?"

Tina squeezes my arm. "Muscle power will actually help you 'cause they won't be able to avoid you."

"Ohhhh."

We get out of the access tunnel about two corridors from the apartment. She watches me close the hatch from the outside, and then lets me keep the multitool.

"I'll want it back when you don't need it anymore, Dumanny."

I don't say anything, 'cause she gives me a peck on the cheek. I can feel myself blushing. If my friends back in Metoronto saw that, they'd give me a hard time. She lopes off in the easy manner of those who've adapted to the moon's lesser gravity. I wish I could do that moongait too.

Dad is waiting for me when I come in and oh boy he

looks pretty angry. He holds up the pressure suit that I didn't put on that morning. I had hoped the lack of it would help me move better and allow me to hit that suck-faced Jordan.

"Manfred Acteon," he says. He only calls me Manfred when I'm in trouble. "I expect you have a reasonable explanation for this?"

Dad grew up in Germany, so he says "reeson-abull." Longer. So it sounds like I'm in real trouble.

The pressure suit is different from the kind the other kids wear. Instead of being cool, thin, and multicolored material it's real thick, like an old wetsuit I had to wear when I went white-water rafting with Mom and Dad. And it's *gray*. Dad had his tiny little robots—he calls them *nanotailors*—make this thing so that it feels more like I'm in Earth's gravity. It's real heavy and I can't move in it. The stupid thing makes me even more gormy, even easier for those Trongs to get me.

"I don't want to wear it!"

"Manfred. You will wear it."

He stares at me, and I stare right back at him.

Mom used to sort these things out but since she died it hasn't been much fun with Dad.

"Tell you what, Manfred. We can get the nanotailors to paint it any colors you want, how's that?"

"I can't move in that thing. I don't care what sucking color it is."

"I've told you about that kind of language, Manny. Your mother never would have approved of it, and you know it. You go to your room until you're ready to apologize."

I hate it when he says that. It's true but it's not fair. It's not my fault she died, and I just wish she was here! I don't care if I change. I want to be more like the Trongs and the Drins.

I stomp off to my room, and wish there was a regular door to slam, just like at the house back on Earth.

Dad has kind of a sad look on his face, and I wonder if he wishes Mom was here as much as I do. But I don't come out of my room to apologize. I can't wear that thing or they'll really get me! So, I do my homework. And then I play space-hockey on holo.

I guess I must have fallen asleep 'cause the next thing I know I'm in my bed and it's morning again. And Dad has taken all my clothes away, leaving me only the pressure suit, still gray, and some underwear. I'm really hungry 'cause I missed dinner.

When I get to breakfast, Dad says, "You can still get it any color you want, but you have to wear it. It's for your own good. If you don't wear it you'll end up too weak when we get back to Earth. I'm wearing mine. You know, if they perform as well as I think they will, everyone who visits Luna One will wear them someday. Imagine that, Manny." He smiles, trying to get me to say something. "Soon people may be able to stay for two years at a time. Who knows, some day we may even make it possible for the poor lifers to return to Earth!"

I don't say anything. I give him the stare, try to imagine him giving in, giving me my regular clothes back, but nothing happens. I eat my cereal and stomp out of the apartment. Will those Trongs be waiting for me before school again? Or after? Then I remember Tina's multitool, and rush back to my room to collect it. Dad is taking his weekly shower; he calls it a perk, part of his employment contract with Luna One. He doesn't hear me return as I grab the tool, and head to school.

It takes me way longer than Tina to open the access hatches, but I crawl through as fast as I can.

I'm late for class anyway. Jordan Alvarez mouths the words: "WORM-fed," as the teacher, Ms. Deach, who up til now seemed pretty nice, says that lateness is not acceptable, no matter how slow my clothes make me move. The rest of the class, including Tina, Jess, and the other Drins, laugh. I can feel my face getting red, and think maybe Ms. Deach isn't so nice after all.

But at recess, things are different. Instead of standing alone on the sidelines while everyone plays their weird moon games in the park near the school, Tina takes me by the arm and leads me to a spot away from everyone else.

"Okay, Dumanny," she smiles, and I don't mind the nickname. "Now we're going to 'splain you how to move around in moonspace. And not wallow around like some newbie just landed."

"Explain to me," I correct. Mom always said that it was right to speak good... properly, I mean.

"Yeah, you can be a brain when you can walk properly. Now do what I do." Tina shows me how to control my walk, to lengthen and shorten my stride, to balance properly. It's really hard work, trying to make your legs do something that they don't want to. We practice all through recess and then after school too.

Tina gets a little frustrated because I'm having trouble. And I try to explain that my pressure suit is applying way more gravity on me than she gets from the moon. "I'm not complaining," I say. "Just 'splainin'."

"Keep trying. If you can learn this," Tina says, "then Jess will let you be a Drin."

"What's a Drin, anyway?"

"We're the Smart Ones. Trongs are just the ones who got here first—who are born here—and they think that makes them better. But we know different."

"What if I don't want to be a Drin?"

"Then I'll stop 'splainin' you how to walk and you can just go suck. And give me back my multitool too!"

"It was just a question. I like it."

"If you're going to be a Drin you gotta know the talk and the rules. After you learn to walk I'll teach you the signs too. But only after Jess says you're in."

And the lessons continue, day by day, with me using Tina's multitool and back routes through the access tunnels to avoid the Trongs. And each day, I return home and practice more before Dad cooks dinner.

One day I say, "Hey, Dad? This suit is actually pretty cool."

"Really? You know, we can still color it any way you want. We can even get it to change color all the time."

"Maybe, once the Drins think I'm cool. I'll keep it gray until then. I kind of like the way it's making me so strong. You know, Tina winced the other day when I squeezed her arm."

"Manny, you've got to be careful. That suit will make you considerably stronger than the other children."

"I wasn't trying to hurt her. I was just playing."

But after that he doesn't say anything. He seems to be really quiet all the time now. He doesn't even get mad at me. I think he must be having bad dreams too, 'cause I can hear him yelling at night. I don't know why 'cause he says everything is good with his job, mining. He's using bugs like the ones that killed Mom. I think he should leave them alone, but he gets mad when I say so. That would be better than when he's so quiet, but I don't want to make him mad, so instead I show him some of the cool tricks I'm learning from Tina.

"Look, Dad. See, even in the suit I can stand on my toes. Look. Neat, eh?"

He looks up from his datapad and says, "Very good. What else can you do?"

"Tina taught me how to do this one-armed handstand. It's easy, and I can even push off a bit." I show him. He looks happy for a minute. I can do a vertical leap of a foot, using only the power of my arm. I'm staying strong for when we get back to Earth.

After Mom got killed, I was in a lot of fights, almost every day. A few kids were nice, but they avoided me, like if they were my friends somehow their moms would die too. It was weird to have someone die like Mom did. It was in all the media. Some of the other kids made fun of me because everyone knew how Mom died. Some of the sucking meanest said it was my fault. Because I was so weird. They kept picking on me, after school. Some of my teachers told Dad. So that's when I got the self-defence training. Then everyone left me alone. Bullies aren't interested in picking on kids they can't beat up or scare. But sometimes I think there might have been a better way to do it. Something that didn't require fists.

"So how is the testing, Dad?"

Dad seems really happy that I'm asking about his work. Probably because I don't usually do it.

"We've been trying the nanite-miners on a crater floor near the South Hangar. So far, they've performed well. We've mined a great deal of tritium from the regolith already."

"What's a regolith?"

"It's what we call the surface of a planet. All the material above the bedrock. The nanites are breaking the tritium out so we can use it as fuel for fusion. They're doing a great job, which means we may leave the moon sooner."

"I hope they work just as good as the suit!" I leave the breakfast nook. It's Saturday, and I forget to say "bye" as I run out the door for a full day of training with Tina.

It's so good to see Dad talking again. As I'm running down the corridor in my best moongait, it feels like I'm forgetting something.

The multitool. The back route!

I remember too late. The Trongs are waiting for me at Lock 12. "WORM-fed, WORM-fed," they chant as soon as they spot me. Jordan signals to the other Trongs—about a dozen this time— and they move in for their dance of a hundred punches.

I try not to be scared. I repeat, over and over, the main rule that Tina told me: "Step softly, step softly." I wait for them to come at me.

They can sense that something's changed. Jordan is careful. He sends the youngest after me first, testing my coordination. A few of the younger Trongs, both boys and girls, are able to touch me but they don't want to get close enough to punch me. My fists are flying dangerously close to them.

Jordan signals them to back off and tells his older Trongs, four eleven-year-old boys and two girls about the same age, to circle me. They do, silently led by Curtis this time, who is twelve. The brown-noser looks worried as he tries to get close enough to punch my arm.

They're scared! Just like the times I got the bullies back home.

"What's wrong, suck-face?" I taunt Jordan. "Don't like it

when you can't dance all around me?" I've been in enough fights to know the key is to make the leader look gormy, not necessarily fighting him.

Jordan sneers at me, and moves in to hit me, so he doesn't look like a loser to the rest of the Trongs. It's a mistake not using them to keep me off balance. I stay on my toes and watch while Jordan does a forward flip over my head and lands behind me. Jordan kicks me in the rear as hard as he can, knocking me forward. I keep stepping softly, and I can turn around as I fall. I slip forward, just a real light push with one leg, and find myself face-to-ugly face with Jordan. I let him have a real hard one right in the solar plexus. I do the karate shout and everything.

There is a terrible crack. Jordan flies backward, a look of shock and pain on his face. When he lands on the ground, his body sort of flops for a bit, and then stops. The Trongs are silent as they stare at him, and then they run away. Not that I blame them—that was a bad-ass punch, and they don't want any of that.

I won! I beat them!

Then I get a better look at Jordan's white face, the wicked bend in his limbs. The rush ends when I realize Jordan looks dead. But it can't be! I walk over, still playing Tina's "step softly" over and over in my head in case he's faking it. No. He isn't breathing and his whole body just looks sort of... wrong.

Ohshitohshitohshitohshit... I almost lose it like the Trongs, but I know that would be bad. I walk to the airlock and enter my communication code into the emergency intercom.

"Yes?"

"This is Manfred Acteon. There's been an accident. Lock 12."

"What's happened? Is there decompression?"

"No! No. Jordan's hurt … he's not moving."

"Okay, Manfred," says the operator calmly. "Medics will be there in a moment. Stay calm. Now, what does he look like?"

"He's not breathing, and his arms are kinda twisted…" Nope. I'm gonna lose it too. Suck. I killed Jordan! What would they do to me? I can feel this hot thing pulsing in my stomach, and I think I'm going to be sick. Then I realize that I have to get out of there. I almost hurt myself again as I start running as though I'm on Earth, but I manage to get my arms up and roll out of the fall. I run hard, but controlled, barely doing my moongait, which is on the edge of turning into my old newbie's lurch.

I run until I get to a tunnel near the South Hangar, where Dad's team is based. The entrance to the hangar is guarded by an older colonist, a cranky lifer named Zachary something. But the old man is asleep, so I run past him to get into the hangar itself, where I hope to hide. But it doesn't look so good. The space all seems well used to me. Everything looks clean and bright. The only parts of the hangar that are empty are the parking places for the vehicles that Dad and his team use. Then I hear voices near the entrance to the hangar, and I look for an escape. I spot the airlock, and an emergency pressure suit nearby.

The suit is one of those standard ones we trained with so I know how to put it on, but there's no way I can wear Dad's special suit underneath. I make sure the oxygen canister is full and check the utility belt. I put on the helmet and start cycling the lock. My own code won't work, but I've watched

Dad do it enough times to know his. His code unlocks the door, and I stick my special suit into a darkened corner of the lock.

Within a minute, I'm outside the hangar looking up at the steep walls of the tunnel leading to the surface. I don't really have a plan. I'm just running, because I don't want them to send me away. I know what they'll do 'cause I killed Jordan— they'll take me to the doctors, and then put me in the home for bad kids. The *joovee* hall, it's called.

Maybe I'll hide here until the others leave the hangar and then get back inside. As I look at the rough-cut walls and the smooth road leading up to the moonscape, I feel pretty scared. It's hard to believe there is no air outside, but it's sure easy to believe it's more than two hundred degrees below in the darkness. The only light spills from the tiny window in the airlock and the star-glow at the end of the tunnel. The fear tightens in my chest, squeezing the breath out of me in short, ragged bursts. Then the lock starts to cycle again. Suck, they know I'm out here! Before I realize what's happening, I'm flying up the tunnel toward the surface, looking for a better place to hide.

The surface is bathed in the light of the Earth, which has just risen over the horizon. It looks blue and white, and though not as bright as even the moon would be on Earth, it makes the moonscape real spooky. It feels like I'm in a dream. But I don't stop to watch. I'm running blindly, as fast as the moongait allows me, escaping from them. Without the extra tension on me from Dad's suit, I can really go! I run across the gray desert until the pressure suit starts to over- heat, the bubble of air around me spiking in temperature. A fine mist, and then drops start to form in my helmet. I have to slow down! My breathing seems pretty weird, coming in little gasps and echoing inside my helmet. I notice that I'm climbing to the top edge of a big crater. Left behind billions of years ago. The sand under me is hard, like concrete. I thought it would be soft like real sand, but it's all jagged and pieces of the stuff bruise my feet through the soft foot coverings of the emergency suit.

I climb to the rim of the crater and look around me for the first time. I'm starting to feel a bit better. I can't see anyone behind me. But I can barely make out the dark smudge that marks the south entrance to Luna One. On the far side of the crater, I see a tower—maybe for communications? I should have paid better attention to the orientation tour when we arrived.

The surface is totally cool. Magnificent. For the first time, I think I understand why everyone thinks Earth people are worms. To live here is really hard. It takes something special. I'm not sure I know what, but I can't think about it now. Even in the dim Earthlight they could spot me. My suit works extra hard to reduce the temperature and humidity that came from me running. It makes a bad noise that comes up through the collar into the helmet. I remember something about them saying that emergency suits aren't designed for long-term vacuum use. Maybe I should turn around?

No, they're still behind me. They'll take me to *joovee*. Maybe there is an airlock and habitat at that communications tower? I decide to risk it, taking long moon leaps down the side of the crater, bouncing up every time I hit the ground. Without Dad's special nanosuit, it's almost like flying! I get to the bottom of the crater in no time.

I spot the workers at the other side of the crater, waving their arms at me. One of them runs forward awkwardly, and the others stop him. He thrashes like an earthworm. I realize it must be Dad.

I stop moving. And then it's like the bad dreams. My heart beats like crazy 'cause I know where I am—in the experimental bug mine! Where are they? Would they eat me like they did Mom? That funny feeling comes up from my stomach, even worse than when I realized I'd killed Jordan. Maybe I deserve to be eaten like Mom because of Jordan... Tears start streaming down my face, and I don't care. The suit makes more funny noises, probably 'cause I'm crying. A whimper of fear leaks from my lips, making virtually no sound. I suddenly realize that I'm paralyzed.

Dad is pointing at his helmet like a madman.

What? It's like the space-cold is making me think very slowly. Of course. Turn on my radio. That's what Dad means. I switch it on.

"Good boy, Manny, good boy. Now don't move. They're closer to the center of the crater, making a spiraling pass of the circle. But movement could distract them—they exhibit hunter-like behavior sometimes..."

I cry a bit, though I'm trying to be brave now.

"You'll be okay, son. You'll be okay." His voice sounds weird; he's scared too.

Dad's guys move around to the other side of the circle, closer to where I am. Dad stays where he is, so I won't lose sight of him.

"Okay. Don't move, Manny. We're going to figure out a way to get you free of the nanite zone. Chuck, switch to our code frequency."

Dad and the man in the suit called Chuck talk for a while, and it looks like they might be arguing. My suit continues its funny sounds, trying to drop the temperature and humidity.

I watch the regolith before me, and there's a little line of movement, probably where the nanites are. Suddenly the fear-feelings are gone, and I feel real strange and calm—of course, this is how I can be with Mom. Besides, I deserve it. But then, I think, maybe *joovee* isn't so bad. I realize there probably isn't anyone really chasing me.

Dad and Chuck argue for a while longer, until they're interrupted by the arrival of more people at rim of the crater. Tina, Jess, and Jordan's Trong lieutenant, Curtis. They look at everything and ramble down the side of the crater with an ease that comes from having been on the moon for a long time.

Still listening, I can hear the guys warning the new arrivals of the danger—that I walked into the experimental mine, and will probably be broken down by the nanites, molecule-by-molecule. They also say my suit would be broken down first, all of the hydrogen atoms unstrung from the protective covering. One of them says, "The cold or vacuum will kill him before the 'nites can get to work on his tissues, though." That makes me cry a little more; I don't care what anyone thinks about me being scared.

"Shut up, you idiot!" Dad roars. "We need Manny thinking clearly, not frightened stiff."

Behind all the voices, I can just make out Tina's voice, trying to reach me, screeching to be heard: "Manny, Jordan's going to be okay! We came to tell you. "

"But he's dead! I saw!""

"Manny, you didn't kill him. The medics got to him soon enough thanks to your distress call. Now calm down, and let us get your Drin ass out of there." Jess sounds really calm, like a pilot in a holo or something. Drin? Then I'd made it. I was in. Not that it mattered now.

"Sheissesheissesheisse," I can hear Dad saying in German.

The nanites are coming closer. I can see the little swirl in the regolith as the bugs break down the molecules, just like the miner-guys say they'll do to me. A line of invisible workers must carry tritium back to a central container in the middle of the mine.

The line gets closer to me.

"Manny, you have to get out of there!" Tina shouts into her helmet mike.

"If he moves, they'll go for him!" Dad yells. "I've seen it before. I'll go. I'll distract them, Manny. No! Let me go!" His guys hold him back, stop him from running into the mine.

He starts sobbing. And then something happens to me. I realize that Dad hurts just as much as me 'cause Mom died. He shouldn't have to go through it again!

"I love you, Dad. Don't be sad like with Mom."

Dad really loses it. He starts wailing, and it's abruptly cut off when one of the miners turns off Dad's radio.

"Manny! You're going to have to jump!" Tina cries. "Use your wormy strength. I know you have it!"

"Jump?"

"Yeah, as hard and as high as you can. Jump back toward us—it's not so far."

"Yeah, 'ya suckin' Drin," shouts Curtis. "I bet ya Jordan could do it."

I grin at that. He knows damn well that Jordan couldn't do it. None of the other kids at school could. I'm the only one that might be able to make it. But the safe zone seems pretty far away.

"Hurry!" Tina shouts again.

The nanites are nearly here. I have an idea! I take off the

utility belt and throw it behind the line of miniature miners. The line stops advancing for a moment to investigate, and then breaks down the equipment in the belt.

I bend my legs and curl down, ready for one giant leap backward. Then I jump with every bit of strength I have and throw my arms back, curling my spine just like doing a back dive at the pool.

I totally take off!

It's like I'm really flying. The regolith falls under my feet. I keep my back arched, and suddenly I'm going over, like I'm performing a back flip. Am I going to make it? I'm heading straight up, it seems. Then I can see the line of safety pass underneath me, the astonished 'O's of the mouths of my friends and the technicians through the faceplates of their helmets as I tumble over them. It seems to take forever, and then I land, about two meters behind them all. I hit hard, dropping on my hands and knees.

Tina is right there, smiling at me. Jess follows, and she and Curtis lift me up by the arms, their grips reassuring and approving. "Only a Drin could do that," says Jess with pride.

Dad is there, crushing me in his arms. It's the first time he's hugged me since Mom died.

11

THIS AMBIGUOUS MIRACLE

66 *Alone, among all the cities of the empire, Eutropia remains always the same. Mercury, god of the fickle, to whom the city is sacred, worked this ambiguous miracle.*

— ITALO CALVINO, *INVISIBLE CITIES*

MARCO HAD MISSED the bus once before and had to spend a cold night in the sprawling ruins. He loved the open space, the jagged broken-tooth skyline against the setting sun. He loved the isolation, but he didn't enjoy missing his dinner or spending a sleepless night in the thin, icy air of the mountains. He'd nearly frozen to death. Why their ancestors had decided to build the first city so high, nobody knew. In the thousands of years since the founding of Eutropia, the reasons had been lost.

The bus was waiting, and he got on it with a little hesitation. Ever since he'd been a boy, crowds and enclosed spaces had made him uncomfortable, a mild agoraphobia. It was why he'd enlisted in the Building Corps to begin with: so he could work in the empty desolation of Eutropia's many ruins, refurbishing them for whenever there was a Change.

The bus was nearly full, and Marco sat in front of two old friends from school, Rocco and Niccilo. The two were opposites in nearly every way: Rocco was smart and funny, Niccilo a bit slow and brooding. Rocco was a short man with a big nose and wild hair, and Niccilo was a tall, attractive fellow, whom all the girls loved. Marco was not as tall as Niccilo, and not as smart as Rocco, but a blending of their extremes.

"What a fiasco," Niccilo groaned.

"They're going to do it," Rocco said.

"Says who?"

"All the papers, Marco. The latest polls say there is ninety four percent approval of a Change. Site I is ready to be lived in now. And it is just too beautiful."

"But it's so small!" Marco objected.

"Yeah, it'll be crowded but people don't care about that. They're thinking about the new bedmates," Rocco joked, waggling his hairy eyebrows.

"And the new jobs," Marco said. "The new houses, neighborhoods. New friends, new gossip, new, new, new..."

Rocco looked bored with Marco's old rant. "We've picked a site and we're leaving tonight, if the vote is for a Change. Niccilo's wife is already there with the kids."

"We refuse to be separated," Niccilo said.

Niccilo and his wife Sophia had been crazy about one another since they'd been teenagers. Marco envied them both. Maybe he might find love in the new Eutropia, after a Change. Who knew? The Oracle might know more about making Marco happy than Marco did himself. Maybe the ancient Eutropians had begun the Changes because they understood human nature. He doubted it though.

"Niccilo and I have talked it out," Rocco said. "The first winter will be hard, but if we stick together we'll be able to survive."

"I'd like to go with you," Marco said. "But I don't think I could share the space."

Rocco had been expecting that answer. "It will only be this winter, and then we can set you up in your own home."

"Yeah, but I wouldn't make it," Marco said.

"Then what will you do?"

"I don't know," Marco snapped.

"Don't get angry with me," Rocco said. "You have to do something. Are you going to just let them put you in a job you hate? You're not married, so they can't force a new woman on you, but what right do they have?"

"It has been the way for thousands of years."

"Join us in exile, Marco. We can do it. We can avoid the Corps," Niccilo said.

"And even if they do catch us," Rocco added, "we'll miss the Change. We serve our time in prison, and then we can return to our jobs. Niccilo can return to Sophia... our lives don't have to be different."

That was the other problem. Prison. If he couldn't take living in close quarters with his best friends and Niccilo's family, he certainly couldn't survive prison. "And what if there's another Change after you're released?" he asked.

That apparently hadn't occurred to Niccilo. The tall man looked at Rocco accusingly. There was an uncomfortable silence, and they all looked out the windows. As they rode, they would already be counting the votes. The results would be in by the time they got back.

The bus moved through the single connecting road they'd already reconstructed from Site I in the mountains, through the ruins of Site II that they were currently rebuilding, to the thopter pads they'd made in the rubble of Site III. The bus topped a hill, and Marco looked out over a landscape blanketed with millions of deserted husks of buildings. The day's last golden light cast long shadows. Shattered windows and tumbled walls made the skyline an improbable fortress. Ragged crenellations for imaginary cannon. In the darkening sky, another star appeared and looked down on the massive, almost-deserted collection of cities that was Eutropia.

At the bottom of the hill their bus stopped to pick up a demolition team working late. A few men and one woman got on the bus, looking tired. Their faces were caked in dust and their eyes were red and sore-looking. Tear and sweat stains formed rivulets on their grimy cheeks. For all the dirt covering her, there was something compelling about the woman. Her hair was hidden underneath a bright red bandanna tied artfully around her head. She was probably as tall as Marco's five-foot, ten inches and she moved with a solid grace, except when she sat down in front of him on the only empty seat left on the bus. She collapsed on it, exhausted. A cloud of dust rose up from her clothes. Marco couldn't tell what color they were in the fading light, under all that dirt. He coughed involuntarily.

"Sorry," she said. Her voice was a beautiful contralto; without being throaty or rough, it suggested a sensual nature.

"It's okay," Marco found himself almost whispering. "You've got a dusty job."

She smiled at him—her teeth brilliant starlight—and said, "You've got that right. You work at Site II?"

"Yeah. I'm a wayfinder."

She arched her eyebrows and said, "Well, I won't hold it against you. Not all of us have cushy jobs. I'm Abrianna." She offered her hand.

"Marco," he said, shaking it. Was it his imagination or did their touch linger? "So do you think there will be a Change?"

"Oh, I suspect. All the media say so. What does a wayfinder do, anyway? I mean, apart from having it easier than someone on the demolition crew?"

"I figure out which buildings can be refurbished, and which ones you're going to tear down. Mostly I'm on my own."

"That's because nobody wants him around," Rocco quipped.

Abrianna laughed, but her gaze never left Marco. "Don't you get lonely?"

"No. I like working away from people."

"But don't you find it strange in the ruins? Sad, even? All I can think about is how the people who used to live here are gone. We don't even know their names..." Her voice trailed off as they passed by the remains of Eutropia's first coliseum. It was a magnificent wreck, especially in the last reddish light of sundown. Its few standing buttresses looked like the rib cage of an enormous, primeval whale.

"I think it's beautifully sad," Marco said.

If Marco had tried to say the right thing he never would have, but he had just said the opposite of what almost anyone else in Eutropia would. Abrianna smiled again.

"What are you doing when we get back?" she asked.

The streets were filled with people, singing, laughing; streamers of colored paper and pignatta dolls decorated the walkways. Instead of going home, Marco and Abrianna purchased costumes from a street vendor and then went to a public bath. After cleaning up, they met in the warm pools, swimming around one another in a slow, sensual dance.

They practically had the place to themselves, as the population of Eutropia celebrated the vote. It had been almost unanimous for Change. The first in thirty years—all of Marco's life!

After their bath, they put on their costumes and went out to join the party. Abrianna was dressed as "The Chaste Maid" and Marco chose "The Dangling Man"—two characters from a popular deck of tarot cards. Both costumes had masks that hid their faces. The evening might have seemed a dalliance, but when Abrianna leaned into Marco at her doorway he did not simply kiss her. He took off his mask, then hers, and said, "You are the most magnificent woman I've ever met."

At that moment, a crowd of celebrants cheered at the sight of the two lovers leaning in her doorway. On another day, Marco would have hated the intrusion, but on that night he loved Eutropia, even though he would be losing his job as a wayfinder. Abrianna kissed him tenderly, and her breath filled Marco's chest until he was light-headed.

She giggled delightfully and said, "You must come up to see my flat."

And later, when Eutropia transported itself from its seaside location to the mountains, Marco moved in with her.

They never wanted to be apart, and for six months it was as though Eutropia didn't exist. For the first time in his life Marco couldn't care less what he did for a living, and he was less bothered by the crowds and enclosed spaces of the city.

By amazing chance—Marco didn't believe in fate—the Oracle assigned them similar jobs, both labouring on the reconstruction Site II. He worked with a distracted eye on the clock, waiting for that moment when Abrianna boarded the bus.

The polity of Eutropia carried on without them. The people loved Site I, and there was an amendment to the constitution: It was decided that until the majority of Eutropia decided otherwise, the city would remain in the mountains and expand into Site II when it was ready. As expected, there was an overcrowding problem at Site I. If citizens voted for a Change they would still move to a new home, a new job, a new spouse, a new life, but the city itself wouldn't shift to a new location. Future votes would have two questions: a vote for Change, and a supplemental vote to Move the city to an entirely new site.

The Building Corps grew massively that year, as young people just out of school volunteered to help rebuild Site II.

A year passed in bliss, and Eutropia voted for Change again, but no Move. Marco was not sent to a new job—as Abrianna was—but promoted to supervisor. At first he'd been worried that he would have to work a desk job, but he was allowed to supervise on-site.

Of the two new flats assigned to them, Marco's was larger, so they moved into it. Living together in a tiny flat designed for one person was crowded, but Marco loved being close to Abrianna. His agoraphobia was all but gone. Even though it would mean a bigger flat, they never discussed marriage, knowing they would not want to be separated by a Change. This arrangement was technically illegal, but they were careful not to tell anyone.

Each night she told him stories about the many cities they would visit when they'd saved enough money to travel.

"In far Zenobia," Abrianna told him, "all the buildings are on high stilts, though the city is on a landlocked plain. Their walkways are bridges suspended in the air, and their feet never touch the ground... In the famed canalled city of Anztysia they marry for life and fathers stay with their children until they are grown."

Never before had Marco imagined leaving Eutropia, but now he had visions of these other cities in his mind. What would their people be like without the Change? Could people do just one job for their whole lives? Spend a life with just one partner?

Marco thought so. He could not imagine life with anyone but Abrianna, and the idea that some societies promoted this kind of arrangement was a dream. In living together without marrying, they had become rebels—albeit a less extreme form of rebellion than what Rocco and Niccilo had chosen. Marco often wondered how they were doing, if they were having a grand adventure. The next year's Change saw Marco in charge of an even larger group of workers—a gang that was going to build a monorail from Site I, through Site II, all the way to Eutropia's distant port, Site LVII, where he had lived the first thirty years of his life. It was a great responsibility and he enjoyed it. Abrianna was assigned a job working as a clerk in a medicinals factory. She did not like the job, but she enjoyed it more than the hard demolition work she'd done before.

Earlier that winter, Marco had received a letter from Niccilo letting him know where they were. And would he mind dropping by sometime? They were squatting close to where he was currently surveying the proposed route of the monorail in Site VI. A few weeks later, Marco took his lunch break to hike to the area. He saw a ruined building with a thin plume of smoke rising from it. If he hadn't been searching for them, he never would have seen it. He knocked on the front door and Rocco answered it.

Rocco's eyes widened and he glanced behind Marco. "Are you alone?"

"Rocco!" Marco hugged his old friend. "Of course I'm alone. I would never inform."

"Thank the gods," Rocco said with obvious relief. "Sorry, come in, come in."

"So how are you?" Marco asked. The walls of the house were dingy and decay hung in the air.

"Oh, it hasn't been so easy for us, Marco. You were right not to join us."

"Really? I was just thinking the other day what an adventure you must all be having."

"Oh, it's an adventure, I'll grant you that. But it's not as grand as it sounds. It's dirty, smelly, messy. Frightening. I don't know how to say this right, so I'll just say it—Niccilo is dead."

"Dead? But, he sent me a letter just a few weeks ago."

"Yes. He cut his arm in the ruins, on his trip back. It got infected. We didn't have any antibiotics and I tried to, ah, amputate—" Rocco stopped himself. "He died."

"I'm so sorry. How is Sophia?"

"We're together now." Rocco looked uncomfortable, and tugged at his hair. "Our own little Change. We're okay, but the kids... they're not getting the best nutrition."

"I'll bring you some food."

"That would be wonderful. You know that the Corps chases us?"

"Us?"

"The other exiles. We meet and exchange information."

"I've never met anyone working with the Corps police, but of course I've heard of them." The Change Corps were the secret police of Eutropia; their duty was to ensure their fellow Eutropians didn't try to avoid the Change. "What do they do?"

"Oh, they try to track us down. Or they try to plant spies to find out where we're living. If we live in small enough groups, it's difficult for them find us. We keep on the move. There's no shortage of housing." For Rocco, it was a weak joke.

"I'm so sorry, Rocco. Poor Sophia. Why don't you return? Or go abroad? Abrianna says the trading ships are always looking for crew."

"I've considered it. But there's Sophia and the kids to think about. Niccilo would want me to look after them, and traders won't take them."

Marco felt uncomfortable with his next thought. He said it anyway: "They could return to Eutropia. I doubt that they'd go to jail, particularly if they say that you and Niccilo were behind it."

Rocco nodded. "Yes, I've suggested that but Sophia refuses. She's stubborn, Marco. She won't go back to the city she blames for Niccilo's death. We'll stick it out. They're bound to catch us eventually but until then I want to honor her suffering."

Marco nodded, not really understanding, but appreciating the magnitude of Sophia's grief. He tried to imagine losing Abrianna, and felt a hand gently crushing his heart. "I'll come by tomorrow with some food and supplements."

"We could use some drugs too, if you can get them."

"Give me a list."

Each lunch hour that week Marco brought a pack-full of food, supplements, and over-the-counter drugs to the exiles. At the end of the week, his survey team was moving out of the area, so he couldn't bring more. By then, Marco had seen Sophia and the children. The kids seemed healthy, if a little scrawny, but Sophia was another person. Marco remembered her as a vivacious beauty, with sparkling eyes and a mouth made for laughter. Now, she was haunted and bitter.

"Abrianna and I will be back next weekend with some more drugs and vaccines—she's getting them through her work," Marco said. "We'll see you soon."

The couple made a holiday of their mission: a hike into the wilds of Eutropia. It would take three days and be a prelude to their adventures in other lands. They had talked it over, and decided to accept permanent exile so they could stay together and explore the world. They were just saving some money before they left.

In Site I the weather was bitterly cold, but the sun made for high spirits—they sang childish songs and told off-color jokes from the Building Corps. By midday it clouded over and they walked through the still-standing ruins of Site III when it began to snow. It was slow going. "Why do you suppose the ruins are so much worse in Site III?" Marco asked Abrianna, who was a history buff.

"You should know that, Marco. Remember the nursery rhyme: First Change was careful and the city was glad, the second was hurried and the city was bad."

Marco barely remembered. His recall for names, faces, their stories, had never been good. As they made their way through the mazes of collapsed buildings and clogged streets,

Marco wondered if everything between Site II and the old city on the coast was as dilapidated.

By the end of the day, it was snowing quite hard, and they were still in the foothills. They discussed heading back but decided against it. Abrianna was insistent the children should have their vaccinations.

It stopped snowing by sundown and the sky cleared as they reached the outskirts of Site III. You could see empty ground between III and IV clearly—the snow made a pristine demarcation between the two sites. A visual representation of Eutropia's historical strata. They camped that night in Site III, along the inside wall of an old villa's atrium, warmed by a fire made of splintered ceiling beams. Abrianna told Marco a story about how the people of Anztysia traveled to work on narrow boats that they propelled with long poles, and then they zipped their sleeping bags together and made love. Afterwards, as the fire died they looked in amazement at the spectacle of innumerable stars above them.

"It seems limitless, doesn't it?" Marco said.

"It's like the way I love you," Abrianna said. "It's too big to describe, and at the same time it makes me feel insignificant and lonely."

"How can love make you feel insignificant and lonely?"

"Alongside it, everything seems small. I do. This is an ambiguous miracle—having this love and sitting under these stars is to know an infinite thing that will still end."

"Sadly beautiful," Marco said. He held her as they fell asleep. The walking was easier the next day, and they made it to Site VI by lunchtime. They soon found the derelict house where Rocco and his makeshift family were living. They were greeted by Paolo, Justina, and Alabria, Sophia and Niccilo's children. Abrianna and Marco found themselves in the center of a celebration. Rocco was his old self and even Sophia, who had seemed so bitter the last time Marco had seen her, was in a good mood.

Sophia and Alabria had baked a cake with the latest supplies Marco had brought in. Rocco produced a bottle of something he called *graffa*, an ungodly fermented liquor made from wild grapes that grew in the plains near the coast. They all had a great time, singing and dancing.

By about three the *graffa* was gone and so was the cake. And though they were both tipsy, Marco and Abrianna knew they had to make some headway back to Eutropia before the sun set. They left the medicine and several medical manuals with the exiles, and it was time to go.

Before they could leave, the apartment door burst open. The Corps officers looked like something out of a nightmare, dressed in black uniforms and wearing gas masks. The children were terrified, and it was all Sophia and Rocco could do to keep them from panicking and getting shot. The police ordered everyone to lie face down on the floor. Abrianna and Marco stretched their arms so their fingers could touch. A trooper stepped on their clasped hands before he put Marco into handcuffs.

Marco and Rocco were hustled outside and lifted into one thopter, and Abrianna, Sophia and the children were put in another. The police didn't take off their masks, and refused to talk with Marco, no matter what he said.

Rocco nodded at the Corps officer on the other side of the thopter from him and explained: "They're afraid of disease. That's why the masks."

"That's silly," Marco said. "I haven't caught anything."

"Yeah, but you know the stories people tell about us. They don't call us squats because they like us."

"But they don't understand."

"Some of them do," Rocco said. "Some of them are too afraid to do anything about it."

"Be careful about what you say," Marco said, "I'm sure they record everything when they arrest you."

Rocco was quiet for a moment, and Marco wondered what they were going to do. The news regularly showed squats being brought to the court. First-time offenders spent a year in a special prison. Would they put Abrianna away just for helping him? Marco wasn't sure what was worse, the thought of prison, or the thought of not seeing her for years.

Rocco coughed, and said, "I know I shouldn't say this, but I will. Word among the others is they reprogram you once you're caught—they turn you into good Eutropians, ready for Change."

"What?"

"That's the word."

"Quiet, you!" one of the police officers shouted from behind his gas mask. Marco thought it made him look like The Executioner in an old tarot deck he'd seen once.

Marco got the worst of it. He hadn't reported the presence of illegal squatters in Site VI. He'd brought them supplies. He had "coerced" Abrianna into stealing drugs from the medical factory. He was a traitor to the nation. Rocco got two years. Sophia and Abrianna got one, though they suspended Sophia's sentence so she could care for the children. Marco was given four years. At the sentencing, Marco had a chance to speak briefly with Abrianna. He told her that she shouldn't wait for him to get out of prison.

"I love you," Marco said. "Be happy."

Abrianna burst into tears. If it had been the last sound he heard from her before they locked them all away it would have broken his spirit, but she shouted, "I *will* wait for you, Marco. Always!"

It was a kind of blessing that Marco was considered a traitor, because they put him in a special prison, away from the general population. He had his own cell, and though he suffered from some claustrophobia, it could have been much worse. Rocco had been right about the reprogramming, though in prison it was called "re-education." He was kept isolated, except for the guards and his "teachers," who were there to help him see the error of his ways. They alternated between lecturing him and trying to brainwash him.

For Marco the days were a blur. On the nights he was allowed to rest, before he fell asleep, he imagined the stars on the ceiling of his cell. He felt Abrianna's presence beside him then, as though they were still in their sleeping bags, the last night they had been together.

The days were lost to years. Marco was part of a small percentage of the population for whom the reprogramming did not work, so his teachers resorted to a fallback: electroshock and chemical treatments. They had no wayfinders or means of saving monuments; like Site III, everything in Marco's mind was demolished. His memory became a city without buildings. And then they built him a new one.

In the outside world, Eutropia Changed twice. The city was in the grip of a Change craze, and now they didn't have to leave the beauty of Site I. After a generation without Changes, they came fast and furious.

After her year in a normal prison without re-education, Abrianna was released, on the condition that she would live with Saturino, who worked for the prison system as a minder. She was not legally required to marry him, but Saturino was able to convince her that it was in her interest. He had friends at Marco's prison who could hurt him. What if Marco should have an unfortunate accident? And so on.

Abrianna put in her year with him, and thankfully, Eutropia voted for a Change. Even the loathsome Saturino and the Change Corps had to bow to the law, and he was replaced by another man, Vivaldo.

Vivaldo was an unhappy man, though he tried his best with Abrianna. At least, he did for the first few months. Then he crawled back into the bottle.

Another Change followed, and Vivaldo was replaced by Tristino—a tall, muscular man with dark eyes and black hair. He was a musician. But for Vivaldo, the Change was a reason never to love. Never to give over that essence of himself to another. Instead, he gave that to his music. Abrianna liked him, though for all his physical charms she would never let herself love him. The remainder of Marco's sentence passed while she lived with Tristino, and she was still living with him when Marco's sentence was over. She wondered what happened to her love, to Marco.

Marco was released into the care of his official minder, Divitia, whom he was forced to marry.

His new wife was marginally insane. She was so kind, so cloying, so helpful, that Marco wanted to strangle her. He could not remember his life before prison, not even Abrianna. But even with the holes in his mind and heart and the constant presence of the fawning Divitia, Marco found brief moments of happiness in simple things like being in the open air and walking alone in the early morning streets. He loved to stay up late and watch the stars come out. He did not know why, but he knew they meant something.

Marco did not realize that during this period Abrianna spent all her energy trying to locate him. But the city had millions of people, and the authorities had changed Marco's identity to ensure that he could not be contacted by any of his old acquaintances and thus "confused."

Ten years passed, Change upon Change upon Change. Eutropia had a mania for Change.

When Marco was forty-seven, the citizens of Eutropia decided to Move as well as Change. Site III had been ready for several years and everyone wanted a new cityscape. The day after the vote, Marco was told that his new wife would be meeting him at his new house on the very edge of Site III. For the first time in nearly ten years, Marco felt optimistic.

He decided to walk to his new home, taking a whole day to descend from the mountains to the lower foothills. In the time since his arrest, Site II and III had been completely rebuilt. He arrived just after sundown at his new address, and was happy to see that the lights were on inside. Even though it was his new home, etiquette demanded that he knock, so he did.

Abrianna opened the door and burst into tears. Marco was struck by her beautiful, contralto sobbing.

Marco felt like he'd been struck in the head. In a rush, he remembered lying under the stars with her all those years before. He remembered even what she'd said. He felt seventeen years younger. Suddenly, it was a summer evening with pignattas and colored streamers, and they had just unmasked themselves. They were The Chaste Maid and The Dangling Man no more.

Then they were in each other's arms, sobbing, kissing. They went inside and made love as though for the first time, but even more frenzied, urgent. Afterwards, Marco said, "They did things to me. They made me forget."

"They hid you," she said.

They kissed again, and stared in wondrous silence at each other.

"Rocco says hello."

"Rocco." Marco smiled, but he could not remember who that was.

"He's a programmer."

"Please tell me he's a computer programmer."

"You think it's coincidence that we're both here? Rocco found out where you were. Then we altered the Oracle's programming. They probably won't know until later."

"You are so beautiful," Marco said, tears in his eyes. "I never thought..." He was too choked up to continue speaking.

They held each other. Abrianna said, "I don't want to leave this bed, but now my love, we have to go."

"We have to go," Marco repeated. "But we just got here." He remembered more, but it was just a feeling: "I've been here before."

"I'd hoped you'd recognize it, my love. But we have to go. There is a special thopter leaving for the port tonight, and we have to be on it."

Marco looked at her, and Abrianna answered the unasked question: "Rocco again."

"Though I've arranged the passage myself." She held up two tickets for a trading vessel bound for Anztysia.

He looked at her with wonder as they walked hand-in-hand away from the villa. As they crossed the empty land between Sites III and IV, the glow from the city faded and Marco could see the stars appearing overhead. He wondered what they would look like in Anztysia—would there be different constellations? Would they sparkle more? Abrianna squeezed his hand tighter.

Marco realized that he didn't care.

SYSTEM IMPERMANENCE

"DO YOU REMEMBER PAYPHONES?"

They had been scarce even when I'd been young, but I remembered them. My first time abroad I'd had no roaming plan. I recalled not being able to communicate with my parents for weeks until I found a payphone on the west coast of Ireland.

"Sure I remember, Marcia. Don't you?" I said.

"Barely. But when was the last time you thought of one? Before I asked."

"*I don't know,*" I was tempted to reply, but it seemed like cheating. Marcia wanted to know something real about me. But the memory just wasn't there. Had I actually used a payphone, or was my reminiscence of Ireland a confabulation?

Sensing my frustration the system kicked in. It found and replayed the memory for us both. For a moment we were pinned in time, totally absorbed by the mediascape as the system immersed us in the smoky Irish pub. The rust-orange phone.

"Yes," she said. "Like that. But when did you last think of it, independently?"

"I don't know... I can't remember remembering."

The system began the next mediascape, but I held on long enough to ask Marcia a question.

"When was the last time we touched?"

13

THE CONSOLATION OF VICTORY

IT DIDN'T MATTER what our politics were. Each faculty member was required to attend the ceremony.

After I cleared security, the university's Protocol Officer grabbed me by the elbow and asked me to join the presentation party on the stage. He registered my shock and said, "Well, we have to include our only Nobel winner in the honor party or it would look strange. Don't worry, the Krijgvader's people approved it, Professor Flannigan."

Great. I was going to have to hide my disgust with the whole affair. I took my seat; thankfully, I found it in the back row.

When everyone was seated the President of Hellmuth University, a windbag at the least auspicious of times, took the opportunity to really wow us with his wooden presence. Then without fanfare, a troop of soldiers took up positions in Convocation Hall, looking quite sinister in their polished black impact armor and toting long autopistols. The Protocol Officer announced, "Please stand for The Great Leader, Jans Midren, Krijgvader of the Afrikaner Empire."

People shuffled to their feet. Midren walked into the room. For a man in his late seventies, he looked surprisingly vital and alert. He strode purposefully to the podium and pointedly ignored our president. Midren launched into his speech without preamble or style.

He talked about the genetic superiority of the Afrikaner people as if it were a scientific fact. It was revolting, the worst kind of racist ranting, yet the audience listened raptly. Midren may have been evil, but he had real charisma.

As I tried to ignore the speech I noticed Emily in the front row of the audience. She wore a wig and makeup and pretended to take notes. There was something touching about the little press card pinned to her dress, even if I knew why she was there. The moment before the shot rang out, I spotted her partner, high above in an airduct. With a whine, his bullet ricocheted off the Krijgvader's chest. The dictator was wearing hidden body armor.

The second shot would have struck Midren between the eyes, but his bodyguards were too good. One leapt and took the bullet in the back of his head. Suddenly there was blood everywhere and people were screaming. The security forces found the assassin's position as the third shot went wide and hit the university president in the chest. His look of surprise was the only spontaneous thing I'd ever seen him do. In the gunfire, the hall became a scene of chaos. The audience scattered, glass showering down on them, and blood streamed from the dead bodyguard and university president.

The bodyguards moved around their leader. Emily ran forward, pen in hand, pointed toward the Krijgvader. One of the soldiers realized the pen was a weapon and opened fire. I think I must have been sobbing as the bullets tore into Emily's body, her eyes haunted by failure. Her pen flew through the air, landed on the platform, and skidded to a halt at my feet. It sat there like an accusation.

They'd contacted me on the day of Burton's thesis defense.

Burton was my best grad student, but I had been worried about his chances. I'd never seen him think well on his feet. This was a problem because his pro-British thesis was going to be under fire from the chair of the department, a rabid defender of the Afrikaner Empire. The history department may have put up with my interpretations of the Afrikaner War of Independence because of my academic pedigree, but that advantage was not going to help Burton.

I was in the middle of wrapping up my first-year lecture on the Political History of The Afrikaner Empire when they came into the back of the lecture hall. I recognized Emily as a former student, but didn't know the Native man. Actually, I'd never seen any aboriginal person before, and I lost my train of thought.

"...and so, by the end of 1918 the Great War had claimed millions of lives, and the Afrikaner Empire covered most of Europe... It proceeded to absorb the empires of Britain, France and Germany, and large swaths of eastern Europe fell under its sway . . ." I trailed off.

There was a moment of silence as the entire class realized that two strangers had come into the room. Most of the students stared at the Native man accompanying Emily. A hundred students began talking at once, and I recovered my composure.

"Please people, your attention. We have a few moments

left. Uh, Mr. Jansen, could you tell us what happened next?" I asked one of my front-row keeners.

"Sir?"

"What happened after King George V escaped from Britain to Canada, vowing never to surrender?"

"Uh, well, quite wisely the first Krijgvader Karl Migstern decided not to invade Canada. If he had, the might of the American industrial complex could have been brought against the empire."

"And?"

Sensing new sport in my question, the class brought its attention back to the unfortunate Mr. Jansen, an informer for the administration I was sure, so I didn't feel too badly about bearding him.

"The empire continued to grow in other parts of the world. Asia, Oceania, and the Middle East."

"And what happened to the non-skoonras peoples of the Middle East?"

"Do you mean the kaffirs?" the little shit asked.

"That is not an acceptable term in my class, Mr. Jansen. Consider this your final warning."

"It is a well-used term, Professor."

I just stared at him and repeated my question: "So what happened to them?"

"Well, many of the Middle Easterners were eliminated, cleansing the land for those of the pure race."

"Such as yourself?"

Jansen sat up in his seat. "Yes, not to put too fine a point on it, sir. And like yourself, I would venture."

"No, you are in error, Mr. Jansen. I am at least half-Irish, and so do not fit the Ministry of Race's criteria for purity."

The class snickered, and I knew that I had distracted

them, at least momentarily, from the honest-to-god indigenous Canadian sitting in the back of the lecture hall.

"That is all for today's class. For next week, read the chapters on the Afrikaner bombing of Hiroshima, Canada joining the empire, and the role of détente between the US and the empire since then."

There were groans. Bags were repacked with notebooks, and the mass of undergraduates shuffled out of the room.

The two late arrivals didn't wait for everyone else to leave before approaching me.

I tried not to stare—I'd never seen one of Canada's aboriginal peoples before. They hadn't outlasted the British Empire by more than a few years. In fact, except for one state-sanctioned trip to give a lecture tour in America, I'd never even seen someone with darker skin. Neither had I seen someone so horribly disfigured. He had a long scar that ran the length of his right cheek, over his chin, almost cutting down into his neck. "Sit down, eh?" he said in a soft, deep voice. It was friendly, but it didn't brook any argument. I pulled up one of the chairs on the edge of the podium and sat.

"Hi, Professor Flanigan," said Emily. "I'm not sure if you remember me, but I took your Intro to Western Civilization course, in first year."

"Yes. Yes, Emily. How are you?"

She smiled almost shyly. "This is George Brant. He's a Six Nations warrior, and the leader of the Victorian Resistance in this region."

Somehow, I managed to respond: "I didn't know that we had a resistance cell in Middlesex County."

"It's good you don't know. But we're right under your

nose in Landon, Ontario." Brant had a lopsided smile, no doubt caused by severed nerves.

I'd never heard someone refer to Johansdon by its original name before. "I guess the question is, why reveal yourselves like that? What do you want? And I should say that I have to be at a student's doctoral dissertation in five minutes."

"Yeah, we know, but that won't be happening today," said Brant. "Your student is in the hospital. Food poisoning."

"I haven't heard that. How do you know?" Yes, it was a dumb question.

"Well, we didn't want him stirring up trouble before the Krijgvader gets here, so we kinda' gave him some bad fish," explained Brant.

"He'll be okay in a few days," Emily added.

"Yeah, as long as you help us out," Brant said.

"I don't take kindly to threats, young man."

"Right. But you're gonna help us get close to The Great Leader when he arrives," explained the warrior. "Then I'm going to kill him."

In that moment of shocked silence, a secretary from the department came into the lecture hall and delivered a radiogramme message: Burton's defense was canceled, and he was in the hospital with food poisoning.

After the secretary left I looked at Brant and wondered if his other threats were real. I spoke deliberately: "I can understand why you'd want to do that, but what good will it do? There are other leaders to take his place. You won't get rid of them that way. Besides, you've tipped your hand by appearing in front of my class today. I wouldn't be surprised if that little snit Jansen was running to the Campus Race Officer right now."

"Oh, sure, we know that. We are planning on that. But

the resistance is... it needs..." Brant groped for the words, and Emily supplied them.

"We need a victory."

I understood. It had been thirty years since the Afrikaners had tasted even a little defeat. Emily waited for me to say something, but when I didn't, she spoke again. "We need a symbolic victory. We also need the Frikers to persecute us more."

"Why? What value could that have?"

"It will make it easier to recruit new Victorians. It will make it easier to raise funds in America. It might even wake the people up a bit," Emily said. She was passionate as she spoke, and I could see a glint of admiration in Brant's eye. Were they lovers? Somehow the thought offended me, and I felt a sense of shame. I'd been living under the empire's rule my whole life—at least, what I could remember of my life— and I suddenly realized that I had absorbed their prejudices too.

"We're brave," Brant said, "but there aren't enough of us."

"The resistance has fought the Frikers for nearly fifty years, living in the wilderness since Edward signed Canada over to them," said Emily. "The Americans give us as much help as they can, but it's hard to get anything across the border. That's not the real problem, though. We need to have a successful uprising here in Canada before they can intervene. Otherwise, the Frikers might use their nukes."

"And then the Americans would have to use theirs," said Brant. "That's no good for anyone."

As I often explained to my first-year students, détente was the dominant factor in world politics and economics.

Since the Americans first began developing their own

nuclear arsenal in 1946, the Afrikaners had been unable to expand their empire in the Americas. It had resulted in a stability of sorts.

"What do you need me for?" I asked. "How can I possibly help?"

"Well, you already have in some ways," Emily told me. "I would never have joined the Victorians if not for your survey course. Our class had a Jansen too, and we all understood the sub-text, Professor. You are getting the message across. That's why they restrict your movements, don't let you lecture abroad anymore."

"But we want you to join us," Brant said.

"Join you?" I laughed. "The Staat Polisie have an open policy of surveillance on me. I'd just be a risk to your organization. In fact, you're probably in great danger now, just for being here."

"Don't worry. We'll go. But only when you understand."

"I do understand, but I have responsibilities to my discipline. A lot of my work is about helping ordinary people do better in a free economy. Like they have in America. Even the Frik... I mean the Afrikaners can see the point of that."

"Oh for sure, eh," said Brant. "It keeps Canadians docile, just happy enough to be glad it's not them getting *purified*."

I looked down, and felt my face go scarlet. I sounded like an apologist, even if I actually admired what they were trying to do.

"So we need you to hide us in your office, the day before the Krijgvader visits," said Emily.

I was even more mortified by my next words: "You'll have to make it look like I didn't know anything about it."

Emily looked at me like I'd grown a tail. Brant just

nodded like he'd expected me to say something like that. I wasn't sure which was worse.

They told me that they'd be back the day before the visit, and that I shouldn't change my routine. The only things I did differently were to visit Burton recovering from his poisoning in the hospital, and to drink myself into oblivion that night.

The next day Regional Geheimleier Anders Vanzoor opened my door and walked into my office.

I'd met Vanzoor on a number of occasions, and it was never pleasant. He viewed me as a dissident, though the State had never declared me one. He looked about my office absently, and then sat down with the ease of a dancer in the chair opposite my desk.

"So I hear your protégé's own thesis made him sick?"

I looked at him, trying not to show my contempt. "He ate some bad fish, from what I understand. Is there something I can help you with, Geheimleier? Why do they call you "secret leaders" anyway? I never understood that. You are here. You're not being secretive about it."

"Ah, the professor's redoubtable intellect," mocked Vanzoor. "Stick to economics, Professor." I didn't respond. "Well, as much as I enjoy these verbal jousts, I'm here on business, Professor. I hear that you had an unusual visitor in your class yesterday. Perhaps you are helping this man, and I can send you to study the economics of uranium mining in Elliot Lake?"

"You wouldn't dare."

"But we would. Your precious Nobel Prize may make you an academic darling here in Canada, and lauded by our enemies to the south, but we do not care about it that much. If you are proven to be a danger to the State, as I believe you are, then we will have to get you out of the way. Oh, I know you're very careful about what you say and how you say it."

I'd always thought my office and home were under surveillance, and that cinched it. The secret policeman sneered at me and continued. "Now, who was the kaffir that visited you yesterday?" He stood up and looked at my book-shelves.

"I don't know him. He was with a former student," I said as casually as I could. "She's thinking about economics as a career."

"And the other?"

"Her boyfriend, I believe."

Disgust crawled over his face. "Hmm. I don't have a file on her, which will soon be remedied. Did she tell you his name?"

"I didn't ask. I found his presence quite disruptive, actually."

The second truth may have obscured the first equivocation, but it did not matter. He sniffed, and said, "I imagine a character like that would be disruptive. Well, thank you, Professor, you've been most helpful."

"If you say so."

"Yes. I do. You Anglos always have such a superior atti-tude, despite your defeat. It is curious to me, but it is a good thing."

"Why is that?" I asked, despite myself.

"Because then I would be out of a job. If you were as malleable as the Germans or even the French in their own way, then I would have to find another line of work. I'm surprised such a simple economic equation evaded you, Professor." He turned to leave, and then stopped at my door.

"Remember that I have my eye on you. And a fellowship

for you in Elliot Lake if it turns out you know more than what you said."

He laughed at his own joke and my mouth was dry. I did not try to respond as he left. My pulse was racing. How much did he know? Was that a fishing expedition, or was he just trying to rattle my cage, get me to make a mistake? It made me crazy, to be in such a position! I'd spent my entire career walking the knife-edge, being critical of the Afrikaner regime without stepping over the line as so many colleagues had. His threat about Elliot Lake was not idle. I knew people who had been sent there. Occasionally we got word back from them and the conditions there were terrible. Those not killed "accidentally" underground had about a fifty percent incidence of lung cancer.

I didn't want to admit it, but I was terrified.

I was also ashamed. It wasn't as though I had a wife or kids to protect like so many of the others sent away to die. I'd had the occasional lover. Friends, of course, but intellectual companions more than close friends. Perhaps the reason I'd never taken more risks was because I didn't have those close connections. I didn't have a real stake in making things better. Whatever you may hear about me later I think it was that moment with Vanzoor, more than any other, that changed me.

The afternoon was a write-off as far as work went, and I was still stewing about Vanzoor's visit when Emily and Brant returned. Before they could say anything, I scratched a quick note: office probably bugged!

They understood, and motioned for me to get away from my desk. I did, and they unraveled a sleeping bag. Emily wrote her own note: "Behave normally. Staying overnight to avoid security sweep. Thank you."

I noticed the duffel bag, imagined the weapon inside it. Emily shook her head, as if to say, "Don't look." I nodded sadly, and locked the office door behind me.

I visited Burton that night in hospital, and he was definitely on the mend. I didn't dare say anything to him directly, but I did mention Vanzoor's visit. Afterwards I thought about stopping by the pub for a nightcap, but headed home alone instead.

I had nightmares. Horrible visions of the genocides—the "consolidations"—in Africa and the Middle East.

Apart from my exhaustion, the next day unfolded as I had assumed it would. Security was tight. I'd never seen so many black uniforms and I must have been stopped half a dozen times entering the university. When I got to my office I half-expected to see Vanzoor waiting for me, the corpses of Emily and Brant littering the room. But it was empty. Emily and Brant were gone, and I wondered if I had imagined the whole thing.

I skipped my morning coffee, hoping to avoid more inspections, and any more discussion about the ceremony. The Krijgvader was visiting to present our own Professor Philip Rushton a special medal of honor for his scientifically suspect ideas on racial intelligence. No doubt the dictator would use the faux research to justify genocides in Oceania and Asia, and it made me sick. I only came out of my office when it was time for the ceremony and the carnage that awaited.

The pen lay at my feet, and I felt short of breath. Let Emily and Brant die for nothing, or give them their victory? Do I make a difference?

The stage itself was as chaotic as the audience. Security people formed a wall in front of the Krijgvader while the academic leaders of Hellmuth University ran around like a flock of sheep in terror. I suddenly found the pen in my hand. Yes, it was a gun of some kind, I could see that. All I had to do was point it and depress the button.

I felt outside myself, watching it all happen. In a way, it seemed so easy. I walked through the frightened cluster of faculty and was soon only a few paces from the Krijgvader himself. All I did was point the pen at the back of his head and push the button. The blast of the weapon was louder than I'd expected, even above the chaotic din. There was more blood everywhere, its sickening coppery smell filling my nose. It was overpowering. I fell to the ground and threw up. That made it easier for the bodyguards to kick me.

Unfortunately, they didn't kill me. I could feel ribs snapping, other important bits breaking inside me, and then one of them kicked me in the head. As I started to lose consciousness, I could see Emily lying between the stage and the first row of seats. She was still alive, though I could see she wouldn't be for long. She looked at me, her fingers fumbling to make a "V" for victory. I returned the sign and saw her smile before she died. A black boot came down on my spread fingers and broke them, and I passed out.

I can still see that smile on Emily's face. Her old gutless professor helped bring the resistance their much-needed victory.

That smile helped me bear everything that happened after.

14

THE GALLANT CAPTAIN OATES

TITUS HESITATED before committing himself to the
blizzard. He knew what he had to do; it was his destiny. But
knowing his fate did not make it any easier. He even knew
how they would interpret this last act: He'd go down in the
roll call of human history as a brave man. A selfless hero. He
knew his injury was slowing down his comrades. He was
going to sacrifice himself so that the others might have a
chance to make it to the next supply depot. He could see it
now as though reading accounts of it years later.

The wind moaned in the force-four gale, lashing the snow
like sand against the bruised canvas of the tent. The snow
had crystallized when the temperature dipped below minus
forty. Dragging the sleds through it had been murderous,
excruciating, and Titus could not stand the pain in his feet
any longer. They were black with frostbite.

Scott was a foolish explorer, but it had been the weather
that killed them as much as his bad planning. Titus understood that now. He could not blame, or resent, Robert Falcon

Scott. But there was guilt. Enormous guilt. He staggered to his feet and walked to the exit.

"I am just going outside and may be some time," Titus said. The others did not say anything, though the look in Wilson's eyes was haunting. They were open, luminescent with fear, and liquid with admiration. Titus felt like a coward, and he would carry it with him to the end.

Since they'd lost the race to the South Pole, the fight had gone out of them. They were putting up a good show, naturally, naturally. Jolly brave and all that, but they were going to perish. So now they all knew that Titus was going to be next.

He had long since stopped noticing the raw grandeur of the place. The relentless cold they'd suffered for the past three weeks had torn the last shred of awe from him. That was for the best, now. There wasn't really anything to see except for the swirl of the blizzard. He closed the tent flap behind him and staggered out away from the other explorers forever.

It had been a tough mission. He was glad it was almost over. He was as afraid to die as the others—more. Their collective resilience and stupidity amazed him. He'd only borne the suffering because he knew he would get out, in this final "gallant" act. A light cut through the whiteout, spilling on the ground. A brief lull in the wind. And he was gone.

Back in his own time, the gangrenous tissue was easily regenerated. But he never did field research again.

15

UNDER THE BLUE CURVE

WHEN ELISA SAT down for lunch, Henry Overduin didn't know how much she was going to change his world.

She and her colleagues from the Department of Corporate Oversight sat in Henry's section but he would have noticed her even if they hadn't. There was something different and magnetic about Elisa Taper. The rest of the diners at Le Fou en Mer were unreserved cyborgs. Most of them wore their cranial implants in a showy style that was vogue among the rich but Henry found the fashion tasteless. Elisa's jet black hair was cut in a bob that just covered her implant; it was quite elegant. Her eyes were a startling emerald green, and there was something about the intelligence in them that caught Henry's attention.

She seemed completely natural—just like Henry. Of course, he had no implants of any kind. Even on his waiter's salary he could have afforded one, but there was no point because Henry was non-eact. He had been unable to access the datasphere his whole life. When he was young, the world had begun integrating with it, and now the world was the datasphere. The latest generation of implants let humans access sensory experiences as well as information. It was more real than real, his regular customers told him.

Henry had never wanted to be a waiter; he wanted to tell stories. But he had no audience. Without the datasphere, he had no way to find an audience. There were no books, no magazines, no newspapers. There wasn't a real movie industry anymore, it having been swallowed by one all-encompassing medium. Even conversation had been subsumed by it. The irony was there was a desperate need for Henry's originality in what the Germans called the welt-geschichte—the world story.

But Henry's tales weren't part of it, because he couldn't be heard. At least, not beyond the routine of taking orders and fetching drinks. He tried not to resent his job. In some sense, he was lucky he was able to work at all. Le Fou en Mer wasn't so expensive that a human chef ran the kitchen, but it was trendy enough that the clientele were all served by real humans. In addition to Henry, the other staff that day included two students from the city's main academy. For them, the job was something they would remember fondly after they had graduated to work remotely or dynamically in the datasphere, depending on their abilities. But for Henry it was one of the few jobs that he could hold, all thanks to his faulty, non-eactive mind.

He tried not to dwell on it while he walked over to the table where Elisa sat with her colleagues. He let them know the chef's specials that day, trying to be pleasant, and asked for their drink orders. It might have been obvious that he found Elisa attractive but he tried to disguise it. No matter,

Elisa saw. She asked him his name, and was somewhat perturbed when he completely ignored her routine subvocal query.

Her colleagues received no answers to their questions about the specials, and one of them said, "I say, chappie. It's kind of rude for you to be offline while you're taking our orders."

"I'm sorry sir," Henry said. "I'm a non-eact person, so I can't hear your questions unless you physically ask me."

There was a moment of genuinely horrified silence when they realized that Henry did not have any cerebral implants, that he was fully and completely disconnected.

"That's fine," Elisa said warmly, and smiled. "I was wondering what your name was?"

"Henry."

"Well, Henry. I'm Elisa, and I'd like a wine spritzer."

The other diners mumbled their drink orders, avoiding Henry's gaze, but he didn't care. He only had eyes for Elisa.

By the time they became lovers, Elisa already knew that Henry liked to tell stories. She also knew that he was marvelous at it. She found his lack of eactive ability was compensated by the most incredible imagination. He could tell her about things that she'd never experienced in the datasphere—and you could experience so much there. She loved the strange sensation of listening to his smooth baritone with her eyes closed, and he delighted in finally finding an audience, even if it was only an audience of one.

One night Elisa said, "Henry dear, have you ever thought about using someone else as the conduit for your stories?"

"Someone else?"

"Me. I mean me. Why don't you tell me the stories, and then I'll find a way to get them produced."

"Do you even know how to do that?"

"Produce an entertainment? Of course not, but I'll find the people who do, and see if they'll help me."

"When?"

"How about right now? Why don't I see if someone would be interested in the story you told me last night, about the world where nobody can hear?"

"Well... okay."

Her beautiful green eyes got that faraway look as she dove into the datasphere searching for the right people. Watching her, Henry felt like he was a lower form of life; there was so much that he couldn't know about society. He was a fish, cursed with the vague awareness that there was an atmosphere filled with interesting creatures and stories up there beyond the blue curve of his world, but he could never experience them. His limitation was not sapience, but knowledge.

Abruptly, Elisa opened her eyes and said, "I've found someone to produce the story. They love it!"

She was so excited and Henry so happy that they made love right there in her reclining access chair. In addition to finally getting a story heard, there was money. Though the credit for story and writing went to Elisa, she transferred all the receipts from the sale into Henry's accounts. She was scrupulous about sending all the profits Henry's way even though she did have to adapt the stories so they would be suitable. But she was completely true to his vision, and that was why producers liked to work with them so much.

Henry was thrilled to finally have a wider audience, though he couldn't really know what they thought of his stories, beyond the occasional snippet of actual conversation he heard in Le Fou en Mer.

"Did you experience the latest ElisaVision?" a customer said one day.

"It was divine. She has the most creative mind, and did you see—" the comment was clipped off as the patron switched to subvocal. But Henry was happy, even if he couldn't hear the praise. For the first time in his life, he started to feel like he belonged to something larger. And he had Elisa's love. They spent every night deep in conversation, and he would tell her stories while she listened raptly. He did not know she was recording these conversations so that she could resend the stories to her producers. They were ravenous for new material, and Elisa was developing quite a fan base. And just as Henry's love for her grew, Elisa developed a hunger for those fans.

Their affair blossomed, and it seemed natural that they should move in together. Henry's home was tiny, so he moved his things into Elisa's place. Soon there was enough money for him to quit his job at Le Fou en Mer, though he was strangely sad the day he did. Elisa kept working at the Department of Corporate Oversight, but they agreed that she should move into a part-time position so she would have more time available to make important contacts in the entertainment industry. Henry wholeheartedly agreed that she should receive a portion of the royalties too.

Every morning Henry walked Elisa to her office building downtown. Afterward, he strolled along the river for a while and stopped at a little café to scribble in his journal, an activity that always got a curious look or two.

A few months after they moved in together, on one of his walks, Henry came across a derelict washing in the river. Henry knew the man was either a data-addict, unable to stop accessing free entertainments long enough to qualify for his basic income, or he was non-eactive. He was a younger man, obviously sick and in need of help. Henry didn't see any implants so he approached him carefully. Many non-eactive persons, unlike Henry, suffered from a variety of psychological problems.

"Hi," Henry said as he approached, in what he thought was a friendly way. "My name is Henry."

"I can hear you!" the young man yelled. "I can—" His shouts were broken by a spasm of coughing.

Resistant TB, Henry thought. For a brief, shameful moment, he debated leaving the man there, but the coughing did not stop and it was clear that he was in real distress. There was no one else around so he used his datapad to call for an ambulance, and then tried to help.

A trickle of blood ran down the man's chin as he slumped to the ground, almost sliding into the river. Henry pulled the derelict back from the water and carried him over to a nearby bench that overlooked the river and the ancient parliament buildings beyond. The man was light, probably no more than fifty kilos, and Henry felt ashamed again for his earlier fear. The young man looked into Henry's eyes with a mixture of hesitation and relief. For a moment, Henry felt a connection with him, then it was broken by the arrival of the ambulance. The medibots took the derelict from Henry's arms. He rode in the back of the ambulance with the man, who had slipped into unconsciousness. Henry listened to the sound of the machines, the labored breathing of the derelict under the oxygen mask. En route to the public hospital, the young man regained consciousness. He slid the oxygen mask off his mouth.

"You know they can't hear us, right?"

"What?"

"The others. The eacts. They can't hear our thoughts. Oh, they try to read our thoughts, but they can't. Not like you. You have a glorious psyche, Henry. Lovely stories, but they're wasted on the—" The medibot put his mask on again, and the derelict slid it off. "They're wasted on the eacts. It's just mind-fuzz to them. It fills the void they've created. It —" The medibot put the mask back on, this time with rough annoyance, it seemed to Henry.

The young man closed his eyes, and his breathing slowed down, and finally stopped with a horrible chattering intake that made the mask bounce. The medibots tried to resuscitate him but Henry could see from the readouts that his frail body had given out.

A tear trickled down Henry's cheek, and he wondered what it all meant. And just at that moment he heard a voice in his mind say, "They can't hear us, Henry. That's what it means."

The readouts flatlined and the medibots stopped moving. Henry let himself out of the ambulance when they arrived as the bots prepped the young man's body. He felt drained. He was terrified not by the man's death but because of that voice in his head. So many non-eactive persons lost their sanity and Henry didn't want to be one of them. There was an entire branch of psychological research devoted to the syndrome, and a small therapeutic community devoted to helping those unable to swim in the sea of the world's information.

Surely hearing a voice in his head was a sign that his own sanity was slipping? He decided not to see a doctor. They would put him on some kind of medication. What might that do to his ability to tell stories? Who knew how Elisa would react? That night, he told her a story about a man doomed to lose his identity in a world filled with people who had already lost theirs. Instead of becoming bitter, or angry, the man decided to live every moment to its fullest, to savor everything that life offered him, while he could. On the fateful day when he did finally forget who he was, the moment passed in peace, because he was happy.

Elisa thought it was beautiful and wanted to sell it right away.

"Tomorrow," Henry said. "It can wait for tomorrow."

"No!" Elisa said. "It's too good. That will touch people. Jay will love it." Jay was Elisa's main producer. She used other people too but he seemed to be the one she mentioned most.

"No," Henry said. "That one was just for you and me. Besides, I was hoping that we could go out on the veranda and look at the stars."

"But you can't see any stars but the brightest, hon. There's too much light. It would be better to look at them in —" She cut herself short. Sometimes she forgot; Henry seemed so normal.

"It's okay. I know it slips your mind sometimes." They embraced, and then Elisa pulled away.

"Okay, you go look at the stars for a while, and I'm going to talk with Jay." She left the room, though she was still sitting right there.

The story was a triumph. It was the most moving thing people had experienced for some time, though nobody could really say why. Elisa's fame—and wealth—grew to the point that it was silly for her to continue working at the department, so she quit. They bought a beautiful house together near the river. Henry hoped they would have even more time together, but Elisa spent many more hours in the datasphere. Henry's morning walks got longer and longer.

On these jaunts he would hear the occasional voice in his head, and over the next few months he started to worry that his sanity might be slipping faster. Whenever he heard the voices, they talked about how the eactive were dead to the world. They couldn't hear, the voices said. Henry figured that his long-time resentment of the eactive was finally catching up with him.

One morning walk, about a year after he met Elisa, a quiet female voice said to him: "You know that she's having an affair—several affairs—right?" The voice was so clear, so devoid of psychosis, that it made Henry stop. A tiny old woman was sitting on the bench where Henry had carried the dying man just a few months before. It was the same spot, and he remembered the young man's death. It seemed like a lifetime ago.

The woman may have been a hundred years old, but her eyes were bright and alert. They regarded him sadly. "He was my grandson. It was very nice what you did for him at the end." Henry was certain that the words were hers. Or were they in his head?

"Sit," she said, so he did. The woman had blue eyes. Light blue ovals with flecks of dark blue in them that sparkled like sapphires. Her face was kind, and though her clothes were threadbare, she smelled wonderful, like freshly baked bread.

"Thank you," she said. "You're not bad yourself. You did a nice thing for my grandson. He was never able to accept the way things are, and he was unhappy. Poor, as many of us are. But at least he had someone with him when he died. You gave him that much humanity. So much of it had been taken away. I don't want you to go on thinking you're going nuts. As lovely and romantic as your carpe diem philosophy is, you can't always live every day like it's your last."

She stood up then.

Henry said, "Wait!"

She turned around and smiled at him.

"I need to know how to control the voices and the paranoia," he said. "I need to know what to do next!"

She winked at him and began walking away.

Henry jumped up from the bench and cried aloud, "At least tell me how you know Elisa's having affairs!"

The old woman turned around. "Just because I'm a noneact doesn't mean I can't listen to the gossip! Your girl Elisa is famous. They love Elisa, and all the men in her life."

Henry watched her walk away. He wondered if she'd just offered him confirmation that he wasn't mad—or that he was.

The week after that, Henry convinced himself that Elisa was *not* having an affair. At least, not one that was taking place in the physical world. He had no way of knowing if she was being unfaithful to him virtually, and he tried not to think of it. Though even when they were together, more and more Henry sensed that she was really somewhere else. She responded when he addressed her, but unless he was telling her a story she rarely seemed truly engaged.

So he told her more stories. They came out of him frenetically, almost rapid fire, so much did he want to have her with him. But he had to stop talking sometime, and when he did, she was gone.

A part of Henry's mind told him that he really was losing it, that this obsessive behavior, this need for Elisa's company, was a sure sign. Other parts—or was it voices—told him it was because he still loved her, and that she was falling out of love with him. The voices told Henry that it wasn't her fault, exactly. She was dead in a way, because she didn't really live in the same world as him.

Henry thought about committing suicide but the voices told him not to. He thought he might do it anyway, but the voices always seemed more reasonable than him at those dark moments. Never once did the voices suggest he hurt her.

Eventually, the inevitable happened. "I've decided to leave you, Henry," Elisa said one night after his bedtime story. The blow hurt, even though he had been expecting it. He felt his shoulders curl toward one another, his chest implode, and hot stabbing tears form in the blue curve of his eyes. His lips shook uncontrollably, but he did not cry. He waited.

"I'm going to leave you the house," she explained. "And of course, the royalties for all the stories in production will still go to you, minus my percentage. I know this isn't what you want, Henry, but I can't stay in good conscience. I'm in love with someone else." After a moment's silence, Elisa added: "I still want us to be friends. And I really hope this won't affect our working relationship." That almost broke him, but he bore up well. His heart was tissue paper, but at least he bore up well.

"We'll see," was all he could say. He wanted to tell her that the stories weren't about his need to tell stories anymore, they were about his love for her. About how he needed her. But he knew there was no point in it. He'd lost her to the datasphere, or some dead fiction within it.

The house seemed less empty when she left. At first, that made Henry even sadder, but he resolved to recover. Before he'd met Elisa, he had been stuck in a dead-end job that he could barely stand. He'd never been lonelier. Now, he was alone, but not lonely. When Elisa left, he lost his connection with her, but not the feeling that he was part of something greater. It was a mystery. Something he would need to figure out before he could move on in life.

He continued his walks, and despite the loss of Elisa, his love and his audience, he started to feel better as each day passed. There were stabs of regret. Surely he could have done something to make her stay? But usually a voice within him —sometimes his, sometimes not—reassured him that it had been inevitable that she would leave. When it was another voice, it usually reminded him that the eacts were dead to the real world.

Time passed, and his stories continued to generate revenue. The house was paid for; Henry knew money would never be a problem.

A year after their break up, Elisa dropped by to chat with him. "I was hoping that you'd be willing to tell me a story," she said.

"Sure." He told her about his walk that morning. How idyllic it was to be outside on a sunny fall day. The pleasure of watching crimson and gold maple leaves fall into the river.

It was not the kind of story she could sell in the datasphere. Its subtleties were lost on her.

Henry tried to engage her in conversation, to ask her about what was happening in the virtual world, but her answers seemed incomprehensible. People had taken to wearing other bodies that looked like aliens, or mythological creatures, and the latest rage was a game called phantromorph, the goal being to see who could change the fastest from their existing state to one determined by a virtual intelligence. She tried to describe it to him, but it was as if she were speaking through water, everything garbled, muted and off-key.

"How are your productions going?" Henry asked her.

"Good. I'm still producing things with Jay," she said.

Except it turned out that Elisa had lost much of her popularity since the stories Henry had told her had run out. Her own stories were hackneyed and predictable. She tried to find the voice that made Henry's fiction so vital but her attempts drowned in cliches and overused tropes.

"I don't have any other stories for you right now," Henry said. And it was true. He didn't have any more stories for her. He had more stories; he just needed to find someone else to tell them to.

"Well, if you have any more, I'm sure they'll be well received, and you'll make lots of money. Let me know."

The old woman was at the river again the next day, on the same bench where Henry had tried to save her grandson.

"So have you decided yet that you don't need her?" she asked him.

"Don't you ever just chit-chat?" Henry said.

"Ah, I'm too old for polite conversation. So what are you going to do?"

"I don't know," Henry said. "Find another audience, I guess. Do you want to hear a story?"

"Yes, please!" she said.

The next day, the old woman was there. So were several other people, all of them non-eactive, like Henry. His skill as a performer improved. He could read his audience in a flash of understanding, sense their collective mood. They were quiet as they listened, enraptured. They loved the way he could surprise them. His control of suspense, and emotion, and pathos.

After a few more days, the audience became too big for Henry to stand with his back to the river, so he got up on the embankment above the boardwalk and told the story that way. He got even better as a public speaker, learning how to project his voice, even on windy days.

Most of his audience were non-eactive persons, and that seemed natural. The eactive had their datasphere. They could keep it as far as Henry was concerned. But even the few eacts that joined them were enthusiastic. Henry's stories made the virtual world seem bewildering, futile. Barren as an empty horizon.

The thought of leaving Elisa trapped in it haunted him. So he invited her out to one of the storytimes. The audience had grown so large that Henry had taken to telling his tales in an amphitheater near the river; before the datasphere, people had performed Shakespeare there in the summers. Of course, it had long since become overgrown with weeds, but within a week of Henry moving there members of his audience had cleaned it up, returning it to its former glory.

"Wow," Elisa said. "Look at all the people. I've never seen so many in one place... I mean, in the flesh."

"They're mostly non-eactive, or too poor to own implants," Henry explained.

"Do you mind if I, uh, record, your story? Of course, if I sell it to my producer, I'll split the revenue with you," Elisa said.

"Jay?"

"Jay?" Elisa asked. "Oh, no, I don't work with him anymore. He's retired. In fact, he's spending all his time in the datasphere now."

"What do you mean?"

"Oh, there are a few people who are doing it. They're extremely wealthy, of course, because they need a staff of medical bots to take care of their body while their minds are free."

"Free?" Henry shuddered.

"Yes. He'll never have to eat or sleep or walk around again."

Henry didn't have anything to say to that, but he thought he could hear the old woman's voice: "Yes, that sounds like hell to me, too."

"Well, I hope you enjoy the story."

Henry got up on the stage, and told an old story about a princess who had been enchanted by an evil wizard. He put her into a sleep so deep that her dreams became her reality, and she became captive. But no prince could simply come and kiss her and so rescue her from her virtual prison; all he could do was whisper in her ear while she slept, and hope that she could hear. She would have to rescue herself.

As Elisa listened to Henry Overduin's story, she realized that she was listening to a great artist. He kept them all on the edge of their seats with nothing but his voice. She knew she was listening to something deep, and affecting, but she had no idea how much this story was going to change the world.

16

COURAGE TRANSLATED

THE LION just popped into the duty-free shop. One moment I was watching my suspect through the store window, pretending that I was looking at a new line of holographic cosmetics, and the next, there was a lion—a fully grown male—standing there.

For a fraction of a second, the well-to-do shoppers waiting for their flights at Mulroney International were delighted. *A lion*, you could almost hear them thinking, *what a charming promotional idea*. Then it roared and turned on the nearest person, an elderly woman looking at a set of Brazilian dataglasses. One rake of its claws was enough to cut off her scream and fill the air with the coppery scent of death. The crowd shouted and ran, which was precisely the wrong thing to do with an aggressive and confused animal. It hunted the loudest of the terrified crowd, and killed again.

I was at the airport for sub-orbital craft near Metoronto following a young fem doctor. She was suspected of illegally treating wealthy patients with a gene-resequencing protocol owned by one of our employers, Thai Biogenics. That file unexpectedly closed when the lion killed her next. Then the beast was outside the shop. It ran past me, following the crowd as it flowed down the corridor toward the security check.

I wasn't rated to carry arms, so there was little I could do. Not that I could have done anything anyway. A simian terror gripped me, an instinctive response that, in lieu of sending me scampering up a tree, paralyzed me. I can still remember the look of shock staring at me from the glass display case, my plain-Jane face set in a mask of disbelief and horror. I'm not sure what was more shocking: the fact that a lion was there, or the fact that I froze. I'd always thought I'd been compensated for my homely square jaw and widely set eyes with an unnatural bravery.

"What a brave girl!"

I'd loved hearing those words growing up. It didn't really matter who said it: when the doctors gave me my universal virus vaccination (UVV) and I didn't cry, or when the teachers commended me for not screaming that time I broke my arm. Though of course, I think I liked those words best when my Daddy said them.

Daddy was the Bravest Man in the World. He was a Protector, a medical officer with the BioForce, back when their job was to protect people from dangerous biotechnology and new diseases, before the way it is now.

I remember the last time he said those coveted words to me. I had been playing outside our house in Orillia, a little bedroom community north of Metoronto on Lake Simcoe, and that meanie Billy Neal had called me Gruesome Gracey and pushed me down. Did I cry? No, I got up and pushed him down.

"What a brave girl, Grace," Daddy had said. "But sometimes force isn't the only way."

That was before he died in Africa. He had been working there after an Ebola-like pathogen ravaged the continent. This was before the invention of UVV. The disease had a horrific death rate, close to ninety-eight percent. It left Africa mostly uninhabited. He had been there, doing research on the disease, but instead of just studying it he had caught it. It was an accident, they said, though my mother hadn't explained it to me at the time. Instead, she'd said a lion had killed him. Maybe she thought that would be easier for a little girl to hear than the truth.

The Ebola-like pathogen ravaged his vascular system and he bled to death. Maybe she thought I wouldn't understand what this new strain was, or she thought it would scare me more. But it was really her own fear at work. In those days, before the UVV, they never knew when a new strain of some terrible disease would kill millions. But to a little girl, the thought of my Brave Daddy getting eaten by a lion was much more immediate and easy to imagine than the microbial world. I used to watch documentaries about how African wildlife was filling in the ecological niches left in the absence of humanity. Almost all of the humans were gone from the continent. There were more lions in Africa then than at any time in recorded history. After Daddy died, I couldn't watch them anymore. They terrified me.

At the funeral, I was a Really Brave Girl. The minister said so.

When I got a little older, and learned what had really happened, I understood why Mom had said what she'd said. But the truth didn't change my goal: I wanted to be a biocop like my Daddy. I wanted to protect people from diseases like the one that had wiped out Africa and killed him. But being brave wasn't good enough. By the time I got through university, you had to know someone in the BioForce to get in, and nobody remembered my father. The best I could manage was to join a private investigation firm that specialized in genetic copyright violation. Which is how I happened to be in the airport when the lion attacked.

The thought of how disappointed my Daddy would be was rushing through my head, slowly easing me back from my fear. A moment later I could hear the high-pitched whine of flechettes ripping through flesh, and an agonized howl from the lion. It had killed seven people, including my suspect, and it had only taken a minute and a half.

When I heard it die, I could move again. Then I immediately went to help the wounded. What a good girl. What a brave girl! Not that there was much I could do. The animal had been an efficient killer. My suspect was quite dead, blood still pumping slowly out of her ravaged throat in final arterial jerks. One victim survived. I managed to tourniquet his thigh wound, to stop the bleeding before he died too. Then I noticed the shelves, where the lion had appeared. Everything on the shelves was gone—the food, the packaging, even parts of the shelves themselves. Like acid had eaten everything away. The sight was a startling one, but when I saw the bomb, I forgot all about it. It was a quaint attack, in an age of biological terrors. By the time I discovered the device, response teams and ambulances had been pouring into the shopping area of the airport for some time. My warning gave everyone just enough time to get to a safe distance. The bomb experts never made it to the site before the thermal detonation. Everything within a thirty-meter radius was incinerated.

But it was the lion that caught everyone's attention. Especially that of BioForce, which was in charge of the investigation. BioForce was the paramilitary arm of the Confederacy of Corporations, an alliance of multinationals who had taken over the rule of failed states and those that didn't want to become failed states. Even venerable democracies had turned over bio-hazard and counter-terrorism policing to BioForce. The unit also enforced Confederacy regulations on new technologies. And they scented one in this case. As a PI, and an eyewitness, I spent the next few weeks on the hot seat with BioForce.

The people in charge pumped me for every conceivable detail about that day, except how I had frozen during the attack. I thought it never would have occurred to them that a fem in such a low-prestige position like mine would try to hold anything back To tell the truth, I was so ashamed that I wanted to hide my cowardice. I almost told them, but I resisted the impulse.

One of the investigators was an extremely prim—attractive in a severe East Indian way, but definitely prim—psychologist named Dr. Amansa. She knew I was hiding something. She couldn't figure out what, and that made Bioforce more interested in me. Particularly the BioForce inspector in charge, a sallow man with a sneering smile and hard eyes named Callow Kirkley. I'd taken an honest dislike to the man, not only because he was condescending and cruel, but because he treated Amansa like a servant. He was the kind of guy that normally would look at me once and dismiss me, I knew, because I was not attractive—but he should have treated her with a little more respect. She and Kirkley were interviewing me for the nth time when an underling poked his head in the door and said, "Turn on the video. It's Africa Now."

He mispronounced it. AfricaNow! was a splinter group of the Gaians, who thought that Africa should be left to restore itself to a natural balance, free from human interference. They had always been non-violent but their spokesfem was explaining their change of heart.

"AfricaNow! has decided we cannot engage in peaceful tactics while the corporations," she spit out the word with disdain, "ravage the Goddess with impunity."

The woman was wearing the robes of a Gaian Priestess. But I didn't notice that so much. There was something about her. She exuded confidence and integrity. She was voluptuous —I'd heard the Gaians were a religious organization based on a scientific theory, but there was something sensual, not scientific, about the woman. I shook myself from my reverie and listened closely to her words, trying to distance myself from her emotive, persuasive speech.

"Our demands are simple. Africa must not be recolonized or settled. That includes small resource missions from any of the corporations. If we can put a four hundred kilo cat into one of your most secure airports, imagine how easy it would be to place much more efficient killers into water supplies and even the air you breathe." The transmission ended abruptly, and a smarmy presenter came on to gabble inanities.

The goal of keeping Africa wild was supported by environmental groups, but there was virtually no chance of it happening. There was just too much wealth in Africa waiting to be drawn out—the multinationals were busy carving up the continent just as the European powers had done in the 19th century. And the few Africans who had survived the plague wanted to return to their roots, a legitimate goal, I thought.

Kirkley motioned to Amansa, and they left me in the room with the vapid announcer for about an hour. Finally Amansa returned, looking probably as flustered as she ever gets. That is, more composed than I've ever been.

"Well, Grace—you don't mind if I call you Grace, do you?"

""No... Johindhra." I smiled.

She arched an eyebrow—either at the familiarity or the fact that I'd memorized her name when she first flashed me her ID badge. But I did want to establish that I had a brain and could use it.

"Yes," she smiled unctuously. "This woman. This spokeswoman for AN, Laska, her name is. She is known to us."

"Well, that's going to make it easier to find her."

"Hmm. One might think so, but she seems capable of detecting BioForce agents easily. We've tried to arrest her before. Our thought was to commission you as a temporary officer. Though you would only be on temporary service with BioForce, the status will remain on your permanent employee's record. Other police agencies of the Constituency will view your job applications more favorably."

"Why me?"

"Ah. Because you're available, and you've proven yourself at least adaptable enough to deal with the situation at the airport. And to keep something about it from me." She smiled.

"Okay. But what's the real reason?"

"Laska will undoubtably find you irresistible. I say this not to embarrass you. I imagine that you have never found yourself irresistible, no? But it is what you should expect. We have a reliable psychological profile of her in this regard, through those agents of hers we have captured, of course. It will distract her from your mission." I must have looked confused. "She is attracted to, uh, plain women. She will try to seduce you. At first this may seem a little frightening to you."

"Why do you say that?"

"Oh, well... can I be honest with you, Grace?"

I nodded, guardedly.

"You have had very little positive experience with men, no? You do not have to answer. Our psychological profile system is very accurate. But the gist of the matter is that you have never been seduced—properly courted and seduced. I'm sure you've had encounters with whatever men may have been inclined to try."

I was offended by the way she said it, but it was devastatingly accurate. From Billy Neal on, men never seemed to like me in a flattering way. None of them seemed to care how brave I was. Or tough. It was probably the reverse: they didn't like that I was both.

Amansa saw that the truth hurt. "I say this to prepare you, Grace, not to embarrass you. It is unfortunate that cismales continue to be drawn toward such simplistic things as youth, the proper breast to waist to hip ratios and so on. But to be fair, cisfems are also still drawn to similar analogs. Evolution is a difficult thing to overcome." This last point was the only thing she said that made me feel better, but only because of what had happened at the airport. Perhaps I wasn't a coward. It had been some distant evolutionary remnant that had made me freeze up.

The psychologist was still talking. "But I say this to ready you, Grace, for the feelings of uncertainty you'll experience when Laska approaches you."

"So what you're saying is she has a taste for bull dykes?"

"No!" If anything, the subject was upsetting Amansa more than me. I wondered if the primness wasn't an act—perhaps she was homophobic. "She likes to seduce straight cis women."

I grinned, happy to dislodge the queen from her perch of primness, however briefly.

And so, I was sent on my way to track down this Laska, the Mata Hari of the Sappho set. They sent me to Prague, Laska's birthplace, and the last city in which she'd been sighted. It was the last place you'd expect to find a coven of New Agers bent on keeping Africa pristine. I'd never been to Europe before—the airfare was just too expensive for a gumshoe like me—but when the sub-orbital plane came into the airport at *Praha*, I was thrilled at the chance to see the continent.

Laska met me there.

It was going to be a short mission. Other agents were monitoring me, but I forgot about them in that moment. Laska was even more astonishing in person than on television.

I should say that despite consistently poor treatment from men, I'm still attracted to them. Gender is fluid, yes, but it's men that do it for me. Still, there was something about Laska. She was physically beautiful, but more than that, she was lit from the interior, a light that burned from her eyes. She moved with a grace that was sensual and charming. She handed me a bouquet, heady with scent and color. I noticed a number of daisies in the arrangement, flowers that I had always liked. Nobody had ever given me daisies before. Nobody had given me flowers before, except Daddy.

She kissed me on both cheeks, Russian or French-style, and said in an impossibly husky voice, "I'm glad you're here."

"Really?"

"Oh yes. Your presence means that they are taking us seriously. And besides..." She looked me over, and smiled suggestively.

She took my hand and led me to a waiting taxi. There was a confusion of noise behind me, an argument, an altercation, but I didn't realize that it was BioForce, losing my tail. Laska held my hand while she talked.

"We knew you were coming, Grace. And I'm so glad. At last, someone in the BioForce who understands what we are trying to achieve. Independence for Gaia, for her continents." She was holding my hand; did I mention that? Her eyes were two pools of luminous blue, and they held me like spotlights. She could do that with them, she could pin anything with her eyes. I listened, rapt. "We have a very special task for you, Grace. We need you to convince the corporations that we mean to succeed. Can you do that? Don't answer yet. We need to show you a few things first."

Then she leaned over and kissed me. A thrill of excitement ran up my spine, bursting out of the top of my head, down through my... well, things got woozy, and I guess I passed out from some kind of drug in her lipstick.

Lions. I dreamed of roaring lions. I woke up in a bright, sunny room. Light cotton drapes fluttered in a breeze that smelled of the forest. I was not in a city; I knew right away because I couldn't scent the ubiquitous sterility of pavement. I got up and walked out the door of my room, out into a wonderland.

There were lions and lionesses everywhere. The place was an old abbey, but all the cells had been remodeled to let in as much light and air as possible, so it looked more like a Roman villa than a Benedictine monastery. I walked through the enclosed compound in a dream. There was no other explanation, because there were lions nearby and my fear was distant. Fading.

They were not statues. They were real beasts of sinew and claw, silhouetting the skyline and the white arches created by light and stone. Silently, they watched me walk toward the chapel, which was overgrown with cedar trees, roses, and an assortment of other wild flowers I didn't recognize. A few daisies littered the base of the stairs. I walked up. Laska was waiting for me, reclining on a purple couch. Several buckets sat before her with an overpowering odor of decay. I wrinkled my nose.

"Sorry about the smell, but we have some humus here to show you how it works. Watch," she said in answer to my unvoiced question. She produced a handful of seed and poured it on the buckets. There was a slight tugging sensation, a little pop, and then there was a lion standing between us. It purred mightily, rubbed up against Laska, and then sauntered over to me. A thrill of terror swam in my head.

"Go ahead," Laska urged with a smile.

I complied and patted the beast.

It purred again and then like any other cat found something else of interest. I was amazed, and something else too. My fear was transformed to rapture.

"So you see?" she asked.

"See?"

"How we can repopulate Africa with native species? All of them. And then the rest of the Earth."

I didn't follow. "And humans? What about the people who used to live in Africa? Don't their descendants deserve to go back? Who are you to decide?"

"We have the courage to do what must be done. Earth needs a chance to recover from us, from humans. And the corporations are the worst of humanity. They must go. A die-back, the ecologists call it. Evolution. The Gaian Principle. We have outstepped our bounds. If a few millions die now, billions can be saved from the corporations and their relentless greed."

I nodded. I'd seen it. In my father's time, BioForce had been about rescuing lives from horrible diseases. I understood. BioForce wasn't about saving people anymore. It was entirely about saving profits.

"So you will tell them? You will stress our message?"

I nodded again, not sure if I could be brave enough. But it was what she wanted. She came over to me, and kissed me again. This time, I did not collapse. But the charge of excitement flowed through me, and I kissed her back. The lions roaring outside echoed the blood rushing in my ears, as we fell back onto her couch...

When I awoke, it was in a hotel room somewhere. Dr. Johindhra Amansa gazed into my eyes, concerned. "You have suffered two extreme drug overdoses," she explained calmly. "And your judgment may be forfeit." Prim bitch.

I said bravely: "I'm okay. I know what they can do."

It was obvious that her masters were watching from elsewhere. I walked to the window. It was still sunny out, but a new day, judging from the ache in my muscles and the fuzz on my tongue. Outside I could make out the buzz of Wenceslas Square. The drapes billowed in pathetic imitation of Laska's retreat.

I explained how they'd gotten the lion into the airport: new genetic nanotechnology that could cannibalize its surroundings for the elements necessary to create a new form and make it live. Somehow, the DNA was programmed in a way to make the new life form—the two I'd seen, lions—do what AfricaNow! wanted. Dr. Amansa was cool, but I could see the professional worry in her eyes.

Callow Kirkley poked his yellow head in the room and said, "We've tracked them."

"Let me bring them in," I said resolutely.

"Really?" Dr. Amansa asked.

"Really. I still think they're dangerous, no matter how charismatic Laska is, no matter what kind of feelings she can awaken. I warn you, doctor, don't judge me until she's in custody. It's a powerful thing, and... and, nothing... nothing to do with being *plain*."

They let me go. It was a longer drive than I'd imagined, so I guess that first time Laska had really dosed me up, hoping to lose the BioForce tracking systems. It took nearly an hour and a half to drive south into the Sumava hills, through lightly wooded hillocks and fields. Kirkley let me out of the car about three miles from Laska's retreat, and pointed me in the right direction.

It was easy to find. There was only one "abandoned" monastery in the area. Laska met me at the gate. I didn't waste any time. I kissed her, though it wasn't the same as when she had drugged me. It was real. She had thick sensual lips that I'd always envied in other women. They pressed up against my thin mouth, and opened voluptuously—something I'd never really learned to do as naturally.

Breathlessly, I said, "You probably have about three minutes until they're here."

She didn't say a word. She ran back to the chapel—and disappeared forever. The lions came down from their perches and stood around me in a circle, but whether to keep me from following AfricaNow! or to keep BioForce away from me, I'm still not sure.

The lions growled as the troops poured in, but they didn't attack. They lay down and let themselves be captured. Just like me...

BioForce knew that I had betrayed them. And I told them why. Message sent.

What a brave girl.

17

THE LITTLE MOTHER WITH CLAWS

I AWOKE WITH A START, my face cut by trickles of cold sweat. I'd been having the worst nightmare: I was strangling someone. My hands were talons, and fire was everywhere crackling along with a babble of voices. It took me a moment to get oriented and realize the gibberish in the dream was actually the excited chatter of my fellow passengers as our bus pulled into Prague's Florenc station. That was my first memory of the place. Language I didn't understand and my hands still curled in a nightmare.

Kafka famously described the city as a little mother with claws, probably because he could not escape her clutches. The city did not seem motherly. I thought it looked like a neglected opera star, a grand old lady who'd been misused for decades. Her artistry taken for granted, or worse. There was something heartbreaking about her. She had once been so talented, so beautiful, but she had been abused. Jackboots marched over her, and then commissars had a go. Yet the city recovered and returned to the stage. But her claws were no use against spring tanks. Twenty more years of lies sealed the silence

But something survived, and the Velvet Revolution proved it. The country was led by a poet. A playwright. All the city needed was a little tarting up, a bit of ego preening. Yes, the old girl would sing again. Beautifully.

The bus parked at Florenc and as everyone chatted happily about being home—or so I guessed—I realized that Czech was going to be more difficult to learn than French. I got off the bus, and stepped into the cool early morning air. The city was eerily quiet. It was April 1993, and the communists were gone. Even the Slovaks had left the Czechs to their own devices. I remember standing there at the bus station thinking that if only I could be so lucky, if only everyone would just leave me to my own thin, vanishing destiny. I had a daydream outside the Notre Dame in Paris. It was the day after Cora had left. I watched the assembled sweating mass of tourists, believers and hucksters, and thought: I could disappear if I just walked into that crowd. I could leave my passport here on this bench or even better, throw it into the Seine and then fade away. But I knew it would be harder than that. It would require time and money.

All I had was time. But I cashed in everything: My plane ticket back. My Eurail pass. My camera. I advanced as much cash as I could on my credit cards and then sold them too. I traded my passport for an Irish passport, and bought a cheap bus ticket to Prague.

The night before I left, all the backpackers at the Three Ducks hostel were talking about the place while we swilled five-franc bottles of wine. In Prague, beer was ten cents a pint. You could live like a king on nothing! It was the Paris of the Nineties. Prague collected nicknames the way it collected mystique: the little mother with claws, the Golden City, the City of a Hundred Spires, the Heart of Europe... anyone could get lost in all that history.

The Czechs have a wicked sense of humor. In 1993, Kafka's face had become an icon. He was plastered everywhere: T-shirts, posters, billboards, walls, leaflets, and even restaurant menus. The irony wasn't lost on me as his eyes followed me throughout the city. I visited his old residence on the Golden Way. It's a tiny bluish-gray house, nestled under the shadow of Prague Castle. My old bedroom was the same color, and Kafka's place reminded me of home. I was angry at the stab of nostalgia; I was disappearing, not touring. There would be no homecoming. They would never see me again. She had seen to that.

The thought echoed in my mind, and I looked up, stretching back to see the imposing walls of the castle above me. The tiny laneway and the modest homes on it were dwarfed under the massive presence of the castle. Its yellow walls reached up. Its lines of windows looked down on the laneway, and to the city beyond. Suddenly I understood Kafka and his paranoia better: He could always be watched from the castle windows, but was he? The thought depressed me as I returned to my cheap Russian-built hotel. The lobby was every bit as oppressive as the castle must have been to Kafka.

That night I had the most vivid dream. I was at my parents' old house and there was a party going on. It was night and a terrible lightning storm was ravaging the sky. Old high school friends were gathered in the living room, chatting, singing, laughing. My parents and my aunt were in the kitchen, drinking and crying. For some reason, it all sickened me, and I went out into the back yard. It had been transformed, and I was in Europe. There was an aged barn, made of stone and gray planks, and it was covered with ivy.

Cora was there, as she always looked: big-eyed and beautiful. And inside that dream, I remembered another dream, as though the dreams were a set of those nested *matryoshka* dolls they sell everywhere here on the streets of Prague. In the inner dream I was with her in a European city, a city that burned long ago. She was on my bed in that dream within a dream, and yet, I could not save her from the fire. In the first dream, in the old barn sitting in the backyard of my parents' suburban home, Cora and I made love in a myriad of ways: frivolous, furious, tender. And this part of the dream went on for a delicious, long time. A conversation ran simultaneously:

–Why did you do it? How could you? she asked me. –Do you really think you can disappear?

–How could you leave me? I responded.

–I'm here now, aren't I?

We caught up on the years, and in the dream I understood that I'd lost her long before, even though it seemed like it had just happened. Then there was a crowd milling around the barn, bearing torches. They were dressed like peasants, and I realized that the matryoshka dolls were melding, becoming just one dream. The peasants had been setting the city on fire. I got up from the bed, and I asked if they were going to light our barn too, and they said no—it was not necessary.

When I returned to bed, Cora was gone.

I awoke on hard, starched sheets, a sickly pink glow coming from the streetlight outside my window. The room smelled of despair and day-old communism. '

The next day, I found a place to live in Smíchov. That part of town was strictly working class, and set on a hill that was separated from the castle by another rise. Near the summit was a grand old *pivnice*—a beer hall—that was surrounded by a bucolic garden, shady under ancient oak trees. And this pub, true to the Parisian backpacker's rumors, served pints of beautiful unpasteurized beer for only ten cents each. Playground equipment sat in one corner of the garden where children enjoyed the hot spring day. Their parents, seniors, and workers in faded blue coveralls sat at picnic tables in the yard, enjoying the shade and the antics of the kids. From the bus stop opposite the *pivnice* you could make out the splendor of the city beyond Smíchov. You could see the grayish Vltava River and the tiled rooftops beyond. Many of the city's fabled spires were hidden from this viewpoint, but you could see the church at Kutna Hora. It was strange, but comforting. Nobody knew me, yet I was not unwelcome.

And on the other side of the hill, just down the road from the *pivnice*, was an old villa called the Bertramka. Once it was on the outskirts of town, and the villa had its own vineyard. Now it overlooks a small museum dedicated to Mozart, and a derelict Tatra factory at the base of the hill. Mozart's friends owned the villa and let him stay there while he wrote the opera Don Giovanni. In Mozart's lifetime, Prague was the only city where Don Giovanni was a success.

Every Tuesday afternoon the museum would have a little concert there, where they played some of his music. The entry fee included a glass of sweet Moravian wine, and I imagined that I was living in the Prague of Mozart—a city of light and music and sweet intoxicants— not the watchful, scrabbling Prague of Kafka. The sneaky, perverse Prague of Kundera.

But then I would come to the bottom of my glass, and the concert would end and the illusion would fade as I walked uphill to my apartment. The air got grayer as I climbed the cobblestone streets, and at those moments I felt like I wasn't disappearing so much as I was becoming unbearably heavy.

I lived in a three-room apartment in a large home about a five-minute walk from the *pivnice*. For Prague, the accommodations were spacious, but expensive. I would not be able to live there very long, unless I found some kind of job. My landlord had once been a diplomat for the Czech government under the communists. He'd retired before the Velvet Revolution. He had a nice garden, and the fresh fruit and vegetables made him popular with his neighbors, with whom he was generous. He spoke excellent French, so I conversed with him when the isolation was intolerable. On my darker days, I wondered if he had quit diplomacy so that he could be a spy. He was forever in his garden, watching me come and go.

Apart from my landlord, nobody seemed to notice me. I was invisible in the crowds on the subway, on the trams and buses, and walking over the famed St. Charles Bridge. I wasn't the first person to have the conceit that the statues on the bridge were watching me.

I got lost in the old town, winding in and out of the labyrinthine streets, looking for places where I could fade away and forget her.

I discovered that Prague was once a city of magic, the home of the Rabbi Loew's golem, and Rudolph II's alchemists. I was in the broken-tooth graveyard of the Old Synagogue when I realized Prague retained its mystical power. The gravestones were so close together that there wasn't room to walk between each row. The bodies were buried so thickly in the ground that the earth buckled. In that place, I could feel the chill of my plan. I was going to disappear. My family and friends would never see me again. It was sad but necessary because of her. I was pleased: Prague was working its alchemical magic on me.

I discovered where the other ex-patriots liked to hang out, and avoided those places. That would be the first place they would look for the old me. But it was hard. My first impression was correct: The language was a challenge, and it was taking me a long time to learn.

I found a job teaching English, where they didn't ask me questions. They paid me under the table in Czech crowns.

Some days I'd take the subway into town. I'd sit on the train listening to the babble of conversation around me, and I was bathed in a sound I could not understand. French had not been so difficult. Of course, with French I'd had Cora to tutor me; those morning commutes became a battle between alienation and memory. I was vanishing to the outside world. It seemed so, but my memories grew more insistent. I couldn't get her face out of my mind, even as I faded like Prague's ancient sgraffito.

The summer faded too, and became autumn. On the first cold October morning, I decided to walk to work. Steam came off the Vltava, and I became homesick. The smell of burning leaves. Canada geese whistling in a "V" over my head. My plan was ragged because of my own weakness.

I couldn't take it. I needed to surround myself with a language I knew. I had enough money saved to visit Paris, so I foolishly took an overnight train. I would stay only a couple of days, in places that I'd never frequented before—perhaps I could find someone to talk to. As we approached Gare de l'Est I wondered if she would still be in town, and at once regretted the thought. She could not be there. It didn't matter how much I wanted to apologize, how much I wanted to find her at the old places, and rekindle the thing that had burned out between us.

The train stopped and I was back. I'd forgotten my goal. All I'd wanted to do was disappear, but I forgot, or I was too weak. That was my undoing. As I stepped off the train, I became visible again.

Kafka was wrong about Prague—it would let me go. But he was right to be paranoid. They do watch you.

THE REAL PRIMO

WOULD you believe me if I told you Buddha had the set-up all wrong?

It didn't dawn on me right away. One moment I was in my rental car, settling into the long trip ahead, and the next, there were headlights shining in my face. The driver looked up at the last instant, shock on his face. Thinking about it, he was probably texting, or maybe working on his laptop, but he was definitely not paying attention to the road. He'd slipped across lanes, in the dark, doing about sixty miles an hour. His massive truck intersected with my non-upgraded, economy rental car—something like a Chevy Spark—made out of tissue paper and paint. That was the underwhelming end of both the car and what you might think of as my life.

There was a horrible screeching sound of metal and machine disintegrating, a flash of terrifying light and a moment of exquisite, transcendent pain. It was more than just a physical agony; it was a feeling of loss, of absolute tragedy. But also, mixed in with the sadness, a feeling of warmth and love. There wasn't time to remember anything. There was a blurry light, and the sound of a baby crying.

"It's a boy," I heard a male voice say above the wailing baby. "And he has very healthy lungs."

"Congratulations, Mrs. Saluzar," a woman's voice added. "You have a fine, healthy boy."

"Thank you, Doctor," I heard a third voice say. Was it familiar? Yes, it definitely was. It was my mother's voice!

I couldn't see much—a blurry vision of what I imagined to be a hospital delivery room. I was shaking, as though I was cold but I knew I wasn't. The feeling felt second-hand, as though I was remembering the sensation of being cold. I was washed, and wrapped in a warm blanket. Then, I was in my mother's arms. I'd just been born.

My vision swam and, through half-lidded eyes, I saw my mother's face. Fifty-five years younger than I'd last seen her. I'd seen pictures of her of course, but in person she was beautiful. She looked exhausted, but radiant. The nurse took me away, and I heard the crying again. Then I realized I was the one crying. But I didn't even want to cry! I wanted to ask my mother... I don't know. It was weird. Was it nineteen sixty-nine, the year I was born? Or was this something else? But I couldn't talk yet.

At first, it was so frustrating not being able to talk. My body was ridiculous; it wouldn't do anything I wanted it to. In fact, it seemed like my conscious self actually had nothing at all to do with the strange little automaton in which I lived. The body cried, pooped, was fed. It was bizarre and awkward, yet strangely comforting being breastfed.

I'd been racking my brain (my brain?) trying to remember when my mother had said I'd started talking, and I was pretty sure it was early, around the time I turned two. Given the situation, it was hard to tell, but I'd been born in the spring, and now I was working on my third summer, so it seemed likely that I could start to talk any day. That was my hope, anyway.

The two years of infancy had been challenging to my sanity. Can you imagine how boring it is? Sure, for the parents it's all "Look, he's discovered his foot!" and "How cute, he burped," but when you're stuck inside the baby observing, it's not as much fun. My baby body was a little robot, and I didn't have the remote control. It did things of its own volition. Maybe that was a good thing. Could you imagine how terrifying it would be for my parents if I suddenly started walking around and asking to read the newspaper?

I was getting a little stir crazy in there. My belief was that, as an infant, I really didn't have the brain wiring yet to deal with this full-on adult consciousness that was hitching a ride. Speech would be a first big step to allowing that consciousness—me—to get out.

"Ba ba," my infant body said, pointing to the sky.

"Yes, sweetie," my mother said. "We call that blue. Blue sky. Can you say blue sky?"

"Ba ba," I repeated.

"Blue," she said.

"Ma ma," I said, pointing to her.

She melted in happy tears. I was nonplussed. I did not say "mama"—that is, the consciousness that is telling you this story. I didn't say that. The little demon automaton that I inhabited said it. And then it ate a bug. And spat it out. And cried.

By second grade it was obvious I was not going to be able to have any direct influence on my body. In fact, I was getting so used to the idea that I thought of it as "his" body. There was the actual me, Peter Saluzar, telling you this story, and the robot me, Peter Saluzar, who is eight and a horrible speller. Lexicography aside, the eight-year-old Peter wasn't a bad little dude. He was sweet with his parents and his younger sister, open-hearted and full of wonder, and he liked the feeling of sunlight on his face with his eyes closed. (I don't even remember doing that as a child.) And, somewhere in there, the younger Peter had some wisdom.

But, he was also an idiot. He seemed to learn best by making mistakes. I suppose we all do—but some of the mistakes were potentially deadly. Like the time he was playing on the train tracks, or even when he stuck a fork in a light socket. Not to mention the time he got badly burned trying to use the stove. I wasn't just an observer; I remembered the pain from all those near misses. I could sense all the things he sensed, in a detached sort of way, but I couldn't do anything about them. It was frustrating. School lessons were unbearable. Imagine having to watch your idiot younger self learn the times table wrong the first time, and then spend the next six months correcting that initial mistake.

"No, you dope! Peter! Listen! Let me help you. Six times 9 is easy: it's like 5 times 9. I know you know that. 45. Then add another 9!" Fifty-two, he fills in the blank, confidently. Chump. In third grade he discovered girls. He played doctor with a cute little red-haired girl named Sally. It was sweet and creepy all at the same time, watching that little bit of medical malpractice unfold. Remember: I am still a middle-aged man, even if I'm trapped in the body of a little boy.

I felt like a voyeur after that, and then I finally remembered some stuff that was about to happen. Bad stuff. And I realized that I didn't want to be there for that. It wouldn't be for another year, so I put it out of my mind and tried to enjoy the last year of pure, blissful childhood. Grade three seemed pretty good then; school wasn't boring, really. And though Sally and my younger self stopped playing doctor, we entered a martial courting phase in which the boys flicked the girls they liked and girls punched the boys they liked, and everyone pretended that they didn't like boys or girls. It was idyllic.

But there was no escape. The year passed. The bad man hurt young Peter. And there wasn't a damned thing I could do to stop it. After that, Peter's life changed. He didn't do very well in school. He lost interest in girls and sports. He did a lot of reading. To be honest, I didn't really remember those years; I had blocked them all out. The time rolled by. High school came around and Peter recovered somewhat. My family moved that year so there was a chance to begin anew, which my younger self wisely seized.

The past was forgotten, or at least, left alone in that dark place, and the automaton became a person again. Though he would never be the same. Something had been lost. Not lost —taken.

When he sprang back to life, so did I. I resolved to try again, to have an impact on the young man's life. There were so many ways that I could make it better for him. If I could only talk to him, mind-to-mind, there were a few things that he should know. He was young. He was beautiful. He was bright and he could, if he set his mind to it, do anything. He needed to know that all the fears and insecurities he had were shared by those around him. They weren't talking about him—well, sometimes they were—but for the most part what he did and said went unnoticed. He could be bold and he would be glad of it someday. But he was a teenager, and I doubt he would have listened to an old man, even if it was himself.

But I had no way of communicating with him. He was deaf and blind to me and my fate. His fate too. Somewhere up the road, thirty-four years or so, there was a texting trucker with his name on it. Strangely, this gave me some hope. I began to believe that when he died, he would join me in the ride. Or perhaps this replay would end. Maybe this was just a version of having your life flash before your eyes? Maybe I was still being compressed between my Chevy Spark's engine and my seat. Maybe these were memories, squeezing out of my mind like toothpaste from a tube? That too, gave me a sense of hope.

He had few friends, but those he had were good ones. Then his first serious girlfriend. Then others, less meaningful. He did well in high school and went to university. In grad school, he met the woman he would marry and have children with. He started a career thereafter, and the marriage, kids, divorce, and drawn-out legal proceedings began.

It was impossible for me to be unconscious, even when he was sleeping. Sometimes I would try to remember what was going to happen next, and then he'd be restless. Sometimes I would try to meditate or, at least, do what I thought was meditation. I'd taken a Buddhism class in university. In Zen meditation it was "just sitting." I couldn't sit, but I could be still and let my thoughts wash over me until they were gone and something like a kernel of myself remained. On those nights, he slept well.

Time really does go faster as you age. I can confirm it. I felt ashamed about how little I had enjoyed my kids. And I realized that my father had done the same thing. And as soon as I realized that, they were grown up, and headed to university themselves.

And then there I was, in the Chevy Spark. It was almost over. I was thankful then. To whom? I don't know. I'd yet to see any evidence of God. Or Vishnu. Or Odin the Wise, for that matter. (Which would have been cool, though I think that might have disappointed me, to know the destruction of the world was around the corner.)

My own personal Ragnarök certainly was. There was the truck. I could get a better look this time, and yes, that stupid son-of-a-bitch was texting! He looked up, and I could see an expression of pure horror on his face. He might actually have survived the crash, as he was in a pretty giant vehicle. Well, he'd have to live with my death, but that wasn't my problem anymore. Now there wouldn't be any problems. Just silence.

The crash was as violent and painful as I remembered, even at once removed. Things went dark, and I felt... content, I suppose.

And then there was a blurry light, and the sound of a baby crying. "It's a boy," I heard a male voice say above the wailing baby. "And he has very healthy lungs."

"Congratulations, Mrs. Saluzar," a woman's voice added. "You have a fine, healthy boy."

"Thank you, Doctor," I heard a third voice say. Was it familiar? Yes, it definitely was. It was my mother's voice!

I couldn't see much—a blurry sort of vision of what I imagined to be a hospital delivery room. I was shaking, as though I was cold, but I knew I wasn't. I could feel it. I knew I was remembering the sensation of being cold, a second-hand impression...

No, no, no, no, no, I thought. Again?

They cleaned me up and handed me to my mom and I

tried to sense the presence of the devil. Surely this was hell? But no. There was nothing but the soft breathing of my newborn lungs, the cooing of a few nurses, and the gentle whisper of my mother's voice, "Welcome to the world, Peter."

So maybe that Buddha guy didn't have it wrong, after all. Maybe the cycle is just not as pleasant as he imagined. Well, at least I hadn't come back as a texting trucker.

I determined to do better this time around. I'd correct some of the things I'd done wrong. I'd make the life count for more. Maybe it would get me out of the loop. But there was no free will for me. Oh, I was free to think anything I wanted, but I couldn't interact with the body. My body. I wasn't going to fall into the trap of thinking of the body I was riding around in as his body anymore. It was mine.

I tried to jettison all that I knew, and experience things again, as though for the first time. I meditated every night when the body—my body—went to sleep. It helped keep me centered and focused on the goal: to interact with the world. It really wasn't about correcting the past anymore, because, well... was it the past? It was happening in the moment. Yet the moments were ticking by. I was already in kindergarten. God I love finger painting! The squishiness of the paint, the way the bright colors mix together to become other colors— what's not to like? Plus if you make something beautiful then the teacher will like it, and give you a star. And so, I was able to experience things again, not exactly as though new, but close. Not even one step removed. Just a quarter pace.

The meditating during sleep time helped.

I couldn't get over how gorgeous the sky was that summer. How intense the colors were. There were so many shades of green in the grass that my dad seemed to enjoy mowing, the plants that my mom loved to tend in her garden, and the trees. I could lie there for hours and watch the verdant arcs of leaves shimmer in the wind, under an endless blue sky.

Most days I could stay in that state of mind, riding out the childhood days. It occurred to me, just about the summer before Grade Two, that I couldn't hear the thoughts of my younger self. I hadn't tried to listen in until then. But they were a nothing to me, apparently as much as I was nothing to him.

Once in a while, he would talk to someone who wasn't there. I think it was his concept of God, though it could've been me, I suppose.

"Why does the sad happen?" he asked, once.

It startled me, because I'd been having a bad day actually. I was not enjoying the moments as much, because it was coming, I realized. It was nearing the end of Grade Three. Soon the "uncle" would hurt my younger self, irrevocably, I now realized.

Because of the pain in the world, I thought. His eyes started to tear a little. Though I hadn't caused the tears, it felt... related. Then it was time to go to the beach with Mom and Dad, and the sadness was forgotten. For a time.

The intrusion came and went. For me, this time around, it wasn't as bad. I meditated at night. And during the day, when my body's emotions were likely to upset my mind, I was able to meditate then as well. I started to see the emotions as being like thoughts. Like thoughts, they could wash over me, surround me, but always there was a kernel that was not those thoughts or emotions.

I spent much of this second time around focused on this activity. It seemed that this was my chance. When I got to the course on Buddhism again, I tried to pay greater attention, and I realized that the purpose was not to focus on my feelings and thoughts, but to be aware of and acknowledge my thoughts, and denial of the world—right mind—that would be my salvation. And thus I corrected my awareness, and hoped that before the truck and its murderous texting driver came around again, I could achieve Nirvana. No mind.

All of my focus was on this. I almost didn't notice what was happening to him this second run-through. It was an all-encompassing activity. I couldn't use breathing techniques, because I had no control over the body. I did feel his emotions, so I could use those as a touchstone for the real world. Maybe I should say his world. I was able to detach. I was able to drift in the feeling of nothingness. But I never really got beyond the detachment of these meditations, and by the time the screeching of metal turned into my newborn cry, I realized that I'd failed. Nirvana was not the answer either.

"Welcome to the world, Peter," my mother whispered.

Wouldn't it be funny, I thought, if I could say, "Sorry, but this is my third time around, lady—it's getting to be old hat."

I could see the headline: "World's first talking baby says there is life after death!"

Of course, this was not a new theory: the idea that you live your life over and over again.

Reincarnation is a core concept of many religions. But the idea of living exactly the same life over and over seemed familiar. Maybe it was one of the science fiction stories I'd read. I'll keep an eye out for it this time around. Instead of Google, I have time.

So this was my third time around, post-death. Technically my fourth life, if you include the first one. As this one unwound, I could see that a lot of the so-called choices I made were actually non-choices. I tried to interfere. I remembered what was about to happen next, so I created an image of that in my mind, and this did seem to have an effect.

"Whoa," my previous self said, after I tried to show him how to not get his heart broken by Cindy McLean in Grade Eleven: "Déjà vu."

It's funny. As soon as he said it I realized that I used to have déjà vu on a regular basis, and then realized that it was coinciding with my attempts to communicate with the First Me. Let's call him Primo.

Primo was susceptible to déjà vu, but he never listened to it. He could shake it off as naturally as a stubbed toe. And it was infuriating.

This time around I felt Primo's anger. He was an angry young man. He had a chip on his shoulder, even though he was basically that kid full of wonder and imagination underneath. I couldn't change his anger either, even if it affected me less. I also rediscovered dreams. What if I used them for a bit of fun? It seemed that when Primo's consciousness was in sleeping mode, I could run the show. I could make his subconscious see and do whatever it liked. And this was freedom.

That was the only good news about the third time around, up until about a week before the texting trucker. I had an epiphany.

I thought how it sucked that I couldn't explain anything to Primo. Then I realized, I had never tried to explain anything to him while he was asleep. It had only been while he was awake!

Maybe I could prevent the accident. I replayed the scenes leading up to the end. The business trip. The crowded airport. The plane's malfunction and the emergency landing in Pittsburgh. My decision to rent a car to drive to Chicago overnight, rather than catch the next available flight in the morning. That was the point where I could easily change the outcome.

Take the free hotel room. Reschedule my meeting in Chicago and take the early flight. Every night I replayed it. I showed the accident. The crappy rental car. The texting trucker.

I showed the end. And then, I showed a comfy bed in Pittsburgh, an easy morning flight, and a successful meeting in Chicago. Both options, again and again.

The morning of the flight, Primo got out of bed, went to the bathroom and stared in the mirror. He looked terrible. His girlfriend, Tara, came in and said, "What's wrong, hon?"

"Crazy dreams. I can't quite remember them, but they're foreboding as hell."

"Dreams are dreams," she said.

He looked at himself in the mirror and I felt like shouting: "They're not just dreams! I'm trying to tell you, don't rent the car!"

Later that night, when the truck hit Primo, it made me sad to think that he hadn't kissed Tara goodbye before the flight.

Fourth time I sulked. This go around, I decided that Primo was just being an annoying asshole. He wouldn't listen, so what was the point? I watched his pathetic life and I was happy when Death Trucker ended it all.

That was stupid, I realized as my mother welcomed me to the fifth time. The sixth, actually, if you count the first go-round when I didn't know shit. I still didn't know shit, but at least I could enjoy it more, right? It was possible to reduce the feeling of watching a life and live it more like the first time around. The secret was forgetting that you were there, that you'd seen it all before, and that you had no free will or ability to control what happened to you. That made it better, made you feel more involved. It was harder when the bad things happened though. For instance, the family friend and his terrible betrayal was more real this time around.

I felt the loss of my first dog more. The loss of my first love. Loss was more intense, but so was joy. On the whole, it was a better way to go than being surly, and waiting for the end.

My will ruled again in the dreams. I made stories. Adventures. Crazy shit. Anything I could think of I could make happen in Primo's dreams. Early on, I just liked messing with physics. He really enjoyed the childhood dreams of flying—he seemed to like it best when flying was like swimming. Occasionally I'd let him fall just to keep it real. But as his life progressed, I played out scenarios that he'd experienced that day—that material was the freshest because all the memories were right there for the manipulation. And then there were the fictions. He didn't seem to remember them very well, but I enjoyed them more than the remixes of memory. This made it all seem more bearable, and when the end came, I had a momentary feeling of panic. What if this was the actual end? What if this was a final death?

"Welcome to the world, Peter," Mom whispered.

I was relieved. That last bit of fear on repeat six made seven better. Even the bad parts were okay, because they were all life. Existence. I continued to exist, and I had the dreams. The fictions.

And so, many, many lifetimes passed.

I lost count of how many lifetimes. Everything Primo experienced elicited a sadness in me, even his moments of joy. Or perhaps I was simply weary. My consciousness felt thin and stretched out.

And then one day, I just felt like I'd had enough. I'd made up all the dreams I could create. I'd tried to influence Primo's life and that was clearly not something I could do, even with all my tricks and ingenuity. I wanted it to end, but at that last moment—the moment of exquisite pain and loss—there was always a stab of fear. That this was it.

The loss was not just because my life was ending. The loss was more than that, I came to understand. It was an echo from the future, I decided. It was an echo of the grief of those who loved me. There weren't a lot of people, I realized to my great dismay. My children, my parents, who would outlive me, a few close friends, and Tara. I couldn't know for sure because I didn't get to see their sorrow. I could feel it though, and I focused on them. Enjoying the moments of love we shared. (Always wishing I'd been more effusive, more loving, when the opportunities arose, but accepting that I couldn't change that now.)

And when I'd experienced every erg of love I could, from a hundred replays of Primo's life, I knew it was time to go, but couldn't. Always that dread at the end. And then the baby crying.

One day, while I listened to Professor Watts describe the Buddhist concept of how the world is illusion, I noticed, again, how my seat mate next to me doodled. He had written "no self" in the margins of his notebook, next to a drawing of a little chubby Buddha with fairies and Vikings playing electric guitars around him.

No self.

I'd read that doodle thousands of times. But that was Nirvana! Releasing the *idea* of self. I felt the old familiar stab of fear at the idea of non-existence. But I didn't cling to the fear.

I realized I needed to let go of the idea of self. There was Primo. But I was an illusion. I knew, then, that I had been on the right track when I'd been meditating all those lifetimes ago.

When I was spinning my dreams in which there was no me, only an endless series of the idea of me.

So when the crash came, there was no Primo. There was no—

19

EMPTY SPACE TIMES TWO

THE CACOPHONY and rhythm of clacking typewriters made Mrs. Gilbert's typing course memorable. Sophie made it life changing.

Each class would begin the same way. We'd take a fresh, crisp piece of paper, and attempt to put it into the typewriter, properly. This meant it had to be placed on the roller holding your paper, so that it was parallel with the paper blade. Exactly one inch from the top. Mrs. Gilbert would check with the ruler she carried on her like a switchblade, to ensure you were right. And then, a mimeographed bit of text that you would have to reproduce, perfectly.

She would set the timer and say: "Now, ladies." (I was the only male in the class, and I never had the courage to confront her on this issue.)

Sophie and I shared a desk. I had decided to take the class on the advice of my older cousin, Bethany: "You'll be the only guy, seriously. Plus, typing is the most useful thing I did in high school." I was sold at "only guy."

Sophie was way out of my league. She was taller than me,

with dark smoldering eyes and a smile that could cause me to dork out like Ed Grimley. I must say, I may have even typed on my tongue once, 'ya know.

The only other hiccup: I couldn't remember to double-space after a period, which, according to Mrs. Gilbert, "Was just good manners." Many efforts were destroyed because of this failing. It was a character flaw, a deep moral lacking akin to picking one's nose, and worthy of a rap on my hands from the teacher's ruler. That and Sophie's more gentle reminders helped me develop the muscle memory to double-space after punctuation.

So during Mrs. Gilbert's class I learned to touch type, quickly, and I learned to love. Slowly.

Sophie and I became good friends during that class, and our freshman year had a wonderful tempo. We would hang out together on the days when our lunch period didn't coincide with her (cool, popular) friends, and my (unpopular, nerdy) friends. In the spring I finally worked up the nerve to ask her out on a date. She declined. She did so as nicely as she could, but I could see it upset her. She knew what would happen. The beat was destroyed. Her answer was like ripping a sheet off the roller and tearing the paper. All that was left was a terrible clacking in my chest.

Eventually, I managed to get over the heartbreak of unrequited teenage love. There were girlfriends, and finally a first love that was returned. And my cousin Bethany was right: Typing was useful. It certainly helped me through university. I could bang out an essay that looked good in a few hours because of that skill. The first love faded away, but still I needed the keyboard.

To anyone born after 1980 I feel sorry for you. You have no idea what I'm talking about. Mimeographs? Manual typewriters? Ed Grimley? Sure, you've never had the agony of typing an entire page of your essay, only to discover the glaring spelling error in the middle of the sheet, but you also never got the sweet, uncontaminated satisfaction of nailing it. At seventy-five words per minute! And by nailing it, I mean making no mistakes.

Typing helped me train to be a journalist. (For starters, I could skip the required 8 a.m. touch typing class for my classmates who couldn't type forty words per minute. Forty WPM? Please.) Even though I had my own computer and dot-matrix printer (all you Gen-Zers can Google that), I was still way more productive because of the skill.

On my first job in journalism, working for CBC radio, I was confronted by an old-school manual typewriter. An ancient beast that required real depth of character. And finger strength, to get through the triple-ply carbonless torture device called "greens" that would enable you to give a copy of the script to the producer, the host, and the archives, all in one go. Mrs. Gilbert would have loved it, though it did put a dent in my vaunted speed. At the end of the first week my fingers—made soft by years of keyboarding on a computer—were hors d'combat, and I was reduced to using my thumbs.

That is when Sophie walked by, tutting. "If I had a ruler, I'd let you have it," she said.

"Oh my god, Sophie! What are you doing here?"

"Slumming. I'm doing PR for Penguin Canada. I'm shepherding the famous author your host is about to interview."

"She's funny. I did the pre-interview with her."

"I know," Sophie said. Her eyes were as beautiful as I remembered, and it was as if all those years had not passed, the paper had never torn.

"So what are you doing after this?"

Requited love was much better, if not as melodramatic. We dated. We weren't Luddites, so the little love notes we wrote one another were composed on word processors. We made love. We moved in together. We started a PR company together, helping authors and other artists tell their story. Our days had a wonderful rhythm to them. Love. Coffee. Work. Love. Typing. We met one another's parents and friends, and everyone told me how lucky I was. (I knew.)

Sometimes I wished that it had all started earlier, that we'd been high school sweethearts.

"You weren't ready for the real me," she said.

"Sure I was!"

"No, you were only ready for the idea of me," she said, and kissed me on the cheek. "Besides, I wasn't ready for you either."

"But all that wasted time."

"Not wasted. Life has a tempo to it, my love. Ups and downs. Fast then slow. You have to space it out right."

Our days stretched into years. We got a goofy Jack Russell, "Ollie," which was short for Olivetti. Eventually, we would have children, but we were waiting until the time was right.

Less of our time was spent at the keyboard, though it continued to be a bedrock skill. And she still was better at it than me, even after all my years of practice. It's how I figured out something was wrong, even before she did. Her fingers just didn't have the syncopation they used to, and soon she was typing slower than I, and making a lot more mistakes. Sophie complained her fingers just wouldn't do what she wanted them to do. And then she started to slur her words.

It was ALS, or Lou Gehrig's Disease, and it robbed her of her typing first. Her speech went next. Then it stripped her of the smolder in her eyes, and soon, her breath.

The sound of paper ripping out of the carriage. Then silence, as grief stilled my fingers. Eventually, much more slowly than in my teens, I returned from the loss. Life never regained its sweet rhythm that it had with Sophie. But I have good friends and a loving family. Ollie continues to amuse with his zest for life, though I worry about his hips these days.

The visceral clang of the typewriter has been forever replaced by the soft click of the computer keyboard or even worse, the electronic blurps of a virtual keyboard. Double-spacing after punctuation is not only wrong, but an outright annoyance. A signpost of a dangerously aged muscle memory, useless in these days of proportionally spaced fonts and perfect kerning. I can't disagree. The extra space looks odd, especially when typeset on tiny screens. If I'm honest, I think that Mrs. Gilbert, and especially Sophie, would agree that a single space after a sentence is the morally correct way to type now. But every once in a while I throw in that extra space. It reminds me of her.

20

WHY'S WALLY

> *I looked up at the mass of signs and stars in the night sky and laid myself open for the first time to the benign indifference of the world.*
>
> — ALBERT CAMUS, *THE STRANGER*

THE SHIRT LAY on his bed. It mocked him. It compelled him to wear it, but he didn't want to. He hated the shirt. That and the stupid hat.

What if he didn't put them on? That was always an option, surely? He had some other clothes, didn't he? He went to his closet and was mildly horrified to see that it was stuffed with striped shirts, red and white bobble hats, and an assortment of jeans. How had his life come to this? He made his way to the back of the closet, and could find nothing but red and white stripes. Red and white. The jeans were all blue, the same style. Not even brand name.

Wally stared at the bedroom, morning sunshine angling in through the venetian blinds. The light reminded him of

Algeria, dry as the pages of a book. Wally had just finished reading *The Stranger* and it haunted him. He'd been to Algeria, of course. He'd been everywhere.

He had met Camus, too, during his time-traveling days. In fact, Wally had met him while the French philosopher was authoring his other famous book, *The Myth of Sisyphus.*

He remembered the conversation they'd had over cheap wine in a crowded Parisian bistro. "For me, chér Charlie, the only serious philosophical question is this: Is life worth living? The world is irrational, and yet... yet we yearn for happiness and the rational. Why? It is absurd. There is no sense to it. This is the heart of my thinking, Charlie. The absurd is born of our human need for reason and the unreasonable silence of the world."

"But don't you feel as though you're being watched?" he'd asked, not bothering to correct Camus about his name. It didn't matter where he went, everyone seemed to use the local version of Wally. In America he was "Waldo," in German "Walter," in France, "Charlie." Better not to make waves, to blend in. His instinct was to hide in plain sight, so he rolled with it, always.

"Watched?"

"Yes. Don't you feel like you're constantly being watched?"

"God?" Camus had said, a look of amusement on his face.

"God? What? No. People. That people are looking for you?"

"You mean the Nazis?"

"They could be Nazis, but not just the Nazis. I don't know," Wally had said. "They're looking for me, though. I'm not making that up. It's like they're searching for me."

Camus had thought about that for a moment, and smiled

warmly. He had grasped Wally's right bicep, squeezing it like an old friend. "Madness has a kind of freedom in it, though you are in a prison, nonetheless. It is another duality."

And then the crowd had started to thin, and it was time for Wally to go. When he was not absolutely alone, he couldn't be comfortable unless there was a crowd. He only felt safe surrounded by hundreds, or thousands. It was probably why he never worked things out with Wilma. Or her identical twin, Wenda, for that matter. Wally remembered the three of them together, that one night. But three, as it turned out, wasn't a big enough crowd for it to work.

Was Camus right? Was it possible there was nobody watching him? If that was so, then there would be a kind of freedom he'd never felt. He wouldn't have to be so circumspect. He wouldn't have to spend all his time trying to blend in with the crowd. That could get challenging, he'd found, especially in more exotic locales, times, realities... Wally wondered what Camus would have made of his stint in a dimension known as Clown Town. The place had been nightmarish. Apocalyptic. Everyone was a clown, and everything was shaped like a clown. Camus would probably have enjoyed the delicious absurdity of the place and time. It was one of the worst scenes Wally had ever found himself in, but if he had been wearing something other than his stripped shirt and bobble hat, those clowns would have ended up juggling with his skull. He knew it.

So the shirt had saved him on occasion, but it was, as Camus hinted, a prison. Like Meursault, the main character in *The Stranger*, Wally faced the rest of his life behind bars. Though unlike Meursault, his life could be very long.

Wally realized that he was still standing in his closet, naked except for his underwear and socks. Red and white striped boxers and knee-highs, of course. His dresser was filled with them.

He walked to the window and opened the blinds. Outside he could see his yard. It was spring again, though he couldn't really tell you how long it had been spring. The trees were in bloom and bright blue forget-me-nots dotted the lush green grass. He could see Woof's tail wagging strongly enough to shake his whole back end, his front obscured by a bush. The dog had probably found a rabbit or some other creature, helpless, trying to hide.

Wally looked at the shirt and all his other clothes on the bed. When he put them on, and picked up the walking stick, he would be whisked away, as he always was. He looked out at the yard, dappled in the May sunshine, and realized that he'd never been in it. He'd never felt the sod between his toes.

He took off his socks. Slipped out of his boxers, and tried to open the window. It was frozen shut. He smashed the panes of glass with his fist. Naked, he climbed through, cutting himself in the process. Red stripes of blood wound down his pasty white legs, but Wally didn't care.

The grass felt wonderful.

AFTERWORD

You've just finished reading this book. (Unless you're one of those curious people who likes to read the ending first. In which case: "Hi, I'm the author. He was a ghost all along.")

But if you read sequentially, then me too. I'm writing this after reading the final draft from start to finish. Strangely, it was a new experience. I'd re-edited and re-written most of the stories in this collection at least a few times, and in some cases, many times over the years. But I'd never read them in one go, as they're presented in this book. It was an oddly singular experience. I was able to step back and take them in, almost as if they were new to me. Except for the most recently penned piece in the collection, "The Height of Artifice," I can't really tell you what my thinking process was in the creation of these stories. Reading them now, it almost seems like another person wrote them. One of the stories, "The Consolation of Victory," I actually wrote as another person – the long-overlooked Victorian speculative fiction writer from London, Ontario, Emily Chesley. (She is also fictional, but lives in the hearts of the Emily Chesley Reading Circle.) In the first draft there were two other stories by her.

That original iteration was more than sixty stories long. That included all my previously published work, and a load of unpublished stuff that I'd either never finished or that never found a home. It didn't include anything that I'd already published in my first collection, *Pirate Therapy and Other Cures*. I managed to cut that list down to forty stories, which is when Cal Chayce came into the picture. Cal is the insightful editor who has helped me with my work since 2012. He did a form of narrative triage on the forty stories, giving them a green (good), yellow (salvageable), and red (yikes) rating in the spreadsheet. We went with the green stories, and then added a few yellow stories that were really more chartreuse than yellow. Those got the most attention. By the time it got to Donovan Street Press, and the publisher and editor Joe Mahoney, the collection stood at twenty stories.

I've been writing short stories for nearly as long as I've been writing novels. In the late nineties my then-agent had suggested I get some short fiction published as a way of getting my name "out there" while he found a publisher for my first novel, *The Amadeus Net*. I didn't realize how interesting a challenge it would be, compared with writing a novel. At one point, as the rejection slips filled the top drawer of my desk, and then the top two drawers, I wondered if I was just wasting my time. My brother Mike encouraged me to keep writing the shorter pieces. Especially as they slowly found homes in a variety of magazines and websites. If nothing else, it helped my confidence finding editors and publishers who wanted my writing. Mike also saw another value, which I may have missed at the time: it was a chance to play with a wide variety of ideas. I think he may have realized how much of a dilettante I am, before I ever did.

The other thing that I've always liked about short stories is how contained they are. If you have an idea that you want to explore, say, artificial intelligence and what that might do to the taxi business, you don't have to weave that into a giant narrative. You can tackle it in fewer words.

I always find it a little precious when artists talk about process, but I'll power through it. If not in an afterword, when?

Kurt Vonnegut is my literary hero, and I've always enjoyed his description of how he wrote. He described himself as a "swooper." A swooper is someone who lets the story appear, higgley-piggley, in the first draft. I've likened it to throwing spaghetti against the wall. You cook up a batch, start flinging those carbs, and the stuff that sticks, well that's the basis of your story. On a good day, a lot of it sticks, and you have to spend less time on the second draft. This is also called being a "pantser" as in: "writing by the seat of your pants." I like swooper better. It seems less chaotic, more acrobatic and free.

On the other end of the spectrum, many writers might consider themselves "plotters." That means the writer spends a great deal of effort working out the plot of the story, the arc of the characters, and so on, before they even begin. I've tried to write that way, but I much prefer swooping. Vonnegut calls these folks "bashers," though I find that a little pejorative. There's no right or wrong way to create art. But Vonnegut didn't mean it as a put-down, I don't think. A basher fixes one word at a time, one sentence at a time, until the thing is perfect. I think Hemingway might be described as a basher. But there's some romance to that approach too. Just think about Hemingway living in Paris, bleeding on the page, as he told himself: "Do not worry. You have always written before and you will write now. All you have to do is write one true sentence. Write the truest sentence that you know."

Bashing has never really been my approach, at least, not until I get into later drafts. Especially with short stories. Under five thousand words, I've always been a swooper. Though when you're flinging enough pasta around, sometimes you get a "true sentence" just by luck. But usually, they come later. My favorite in this collection is: "The worst form of nostalgia is unrequited love."

The length of short fiction is a real challenge. You don't have chapters at your disposal. You don't even have scenes, really. Each sentence, each paragraph has to count. It has to tell the reader something about the character, or move the plot forward. Sometimes I fail at this. Even some of the short pieces I've had published over the years haven't always succeeded; many of them didn't find their way into this book.

Like a lot of fiction there's a kernel of lived experience in many of these tales, even the ones set in fabulist settings. Those moments ring out to me, but I hope they don't sound any louder to you, the reader, than the rest. Re-reading this collection reminded me of how profound my experience of living in Prague was. There's no doubt it left an indelible mark. I did take a course in Buddhism at university, but that's the only intersection with reality in "The Real Primo." I did, of course, learn how to type in a class much like the one described in "Empty Space Times Two" and I did have to deal with those gosh-darned greens at the CBC, but those are the only parts of the story that are historical facts. I hope they're all true, emotionally, and in the way that Hemingway meant.

For the most part, the stories are presented as they originally were, though Cal and Joe have helped me polish them to a nice shine. (Thanks guys!) There were a few things that needed updating, just in terms of storytelling. The almost complete disappearance of pay phones, for example, had to be excised from a couple of tales. And I had to push the time-frame of "After the Internet" ahead a bit – I do believe a version of that world is coming, but thankfully, not as quickly as I'd originally imagined it. That world is on display in other stories, such as "Under the Blue Curve" and "System Impermanence."

It's a world threatening to be born. But we still have time, maybe not to prevent it, but at least we can still choose to make it more human and humane.

CREDITS

"Wormageddon" originally appeared in *The Saturday Evening Post,* November 2016.

"Close to the Wind" originally appeared in *Far Sector SFFH* (Fictionwise.com), Fall Issue, 2003

"Hounding Manny" originally appeared in *Oceans of the Mind,* Issue VI, 2002

"The Consolation of Victory" originally appeared in *Paradox,* Winter Issue, 2004

"The Gallant Captain Oates" originally appeared in *Would That It Were,* Summer Issue, 2002

"The Real Primo" originally appeared in *Corvus Review,* Fall 2016

"After the Internet" originally appeared in *Western Alumni Gazette,* Fall Issue, 2001

"Under the Blue Curve" originally appeared in *Abyss & Apex,* Fourth Quarter Issue, 2007

"Courage Translated" originally appeared in *TT2000 Anthology,* 2000

"Empty Space Times Two" originally appeared in *The Saturday Evening Post*, May 2016.

"Why's Wally" originally appeared in *Jersey Devil Press*, January 2014.

ACKNOWLEDGMENTS

Thanks to my friends and loved ones who supported me throughout the writing of these stories, especially to my long-suffering beta-readers, Jeff Black, Mike Rayner, Paul Suttie, John Sloan, Scott Hill, David Lurie and the other members of the Emily Chesley Reading Circle, whose feedback has been invaluable over the years. To Mike an extra thank you for encouraging me to write these short pieces in the first place!

Obviously, this collection doesn't exist without the help and hard work of my freelance editor Cal Chayce. If you're a writer or a publishing house that needs help, he is your man!

And a special thanks to my friend, co-host of Re-Creative, and now my publisher, Joe Mahoney. Joe, you're the best!

ABOUT THE AUTHOR

Human-shaped, monkey-loving, robot-fighting, pirate-hearted, storytelling junkie, Mark Rayner is an award-winning author of satire and speculative fiction. He writes in the genres of science fiction, humorous SF and dark comedy. He dips his toe in the occasional bit of dramatic prose and experimental/literary fiction. When not working on the next novel, he pens short stories, squibs and other drivel. (Some pure, and some quite tainted with meaning.)

He does all these things while being Canadian and owning cats.

TRY A NOVEL – ON MARK!

If you enjoyed this collection, then you will want to sample a longer work. Join Mark's mailing list and he'll send you one of his earlier novels!

Plus, you'll get regular giveaways, essays, updates about Mark's writing, and the occasional free short story!

https://markarayner.com/get-a-free-book/